He had kissed her—then he had said he was sorry!

Katie blushed furiously as she recalled David's passionate kiss in the spotlight of the Antilles Lounge. Just as Stan had used her to charm his clients, she felt that David was now amusing himself with her naïvete. Katie was certain that she was a novelty with whom he would eventually grow bored. He and Giselle had probably enjoyed a good laugh together after Katie rushed to her cabin—utterly mortified with the intensity of her own reactions.

And what about that other kiss on the first night at sea? Was it an honor bestowed on the newest member of the travel agency? A memory to pack away with other mementos of the trip? A natural outcome of moonlight and mood music? After all, David was a man, and men seemed to share a number of disturbing similarities.

A kiss was a sacred thing, Katie believed, to be reserved for private moments and to be exchanged between two people who cared deeply for each other. Now she had dropped her guard with David more than once, overpowered by his irresistible good looks. But "beauty is only skin deep," Gran Lucy had often reminded her, and who knew what lay beneath the surface of the dashing and enigmatic David Wallace!

ON WINGS OF LOVE

Elaine L. Schulte

Serenade
BOOKS
of the Zondervan Publishing House
Grand Rapids, Michigan

ON WINGS OF LOVE
Copyright © 1983 by The Zondervan Corporation,
1415 Lake Drive, S.E.,
Grand Rapids, Michigan 49506

Library of Congress Cataloging in Publication Data

Schulte, Elaine L.
   On wings of love.

   I. Title.
PS3569.C539506   1983   813'.54   83-6696
ISBN 0-310-46412-9

Edited by Anne Severance
Designed by Kim Koning

All rights reserved. No part of this publication may be reproduced, stored in a retrieval system, or transmitted in any form or by any means—electronic, mechanical, photocopy, recording, or any other—except for brief quotations in printed reviews, without the prior permission of the publisher.

Printed in the United States of America

85 86 87 88 89 / 8 7 6 5 4 3 2

To my dear Frank, a very great love

There is nothing holier in this life of ours than the first consciousness of love—the first fluttering of its silken wings—the first rising sound and breath of that wind which is so soon to sweep through the soul, to purify or to destroy.

                                     Longfellow

CHAPTER 1

KATIE ANNE THOMPSON sat staring at the sheet of paper in her typewriter, her thoughts on the silken wings of love. The words flitting through her mind came from something she had read about "the first consciousness of love, the first fluttering of its silken wings, the first rising sound and breath of that wind which is so soon to sweep through the soul, to purify or to destroy."

Longfellow. He was the poet who had written the disturbing phrases. Although she wasn't certain what he meant by love purifying the soul, she did understand about its power to destroy. Love had all but annihilated her only months ago, and once was more than enough!

Still, a voice within her whispered: Perhaps it would be different with another man. Perhaps it would be different with someone like . . . David Wallace.

David Wallace, the president and part owner of Wallace-Tyler Tour and Travel, would be driving from the downtown Los Angeles office for this afternoon's quarterly meeting of the board. She suspected that every woman in this, the southern district office, was secretly in love with him. Well, she would not be one of them! She ripped the ruined paper from her typewriter—her third attempt to type the quarterly report.

Slipping a fresh sheet of Wallace-Tyler Tour and Travel letterhead into the typewriter, she typed the date—October 15—her twenty-fourth birthday, and not a very auspicious one so far. It also occurred to her that she had worked here for exactly two months, prompting a new line of thought. It still seemed mysterious that she had been offered this job as office manager on the very evening she had returned from Northern California to her condo in Santa Monica.

Someone from the research company where she had worked must have told Bob Tyler that she had quit her job and was available for employment. Had that person also known that she had broken her engagement to Stan on that same horrid day? That she had fled wildly to her grandmother's house in Northern California for a month to recover?

She typed briskly and accurately, although as office manager, she was required to prepare only the most confidential reports. Scanning the page, she pulled the completed paper from the typewriter.

"All done?" Bob Tyler, her tall, sandy-haired boss, asked as he strode to her desk.

"Just finished." She ran a finger down the columns of figures to compare them with the rough draft. "I finally got the better of it," she added, sitting back with a sigh of relief.

Bob grinned. "Your reward is in sight. I'm taking you out to lunch."

She shook her head firmly, luxuriant sable hair rippling about her shoulders. "Thanks, but I'd really rather not." She didn't want to encourage his interest, nor any other man's for that matter. He was a wonderful boss, thirty-two and attractive, but it was better not to become personally involved with a man who was separated from his wife. It would be dreadful to be the final straw between them, however innocently.

He looked crestfallen. "Giselle's coming along, and we're meeting David Wallace."

All the more reason not to go, Katie decided. The glamorous Giselle Vallon, another owner of the company and its top travel agent, was said to be interested in David Wallace. Katie did not care to watch the predatory female spinning her web.

"It's a business lunch," Bob added. "We'd really like for you to be there."

"Well, then . . . of course." Strange, she thought, grabbing her handbag from a desk drawer. She had never been invited to a business lunch before. "I hope there's time for me to freshen up."

"You've nothing to freshen up," Bob said, cocking an appreciative eye at her, "but I'll give you two minutes. We're supposed to meet David in San Pedro, and you know noontime traffic on Fridays."

"*Five* minutes," she called back, rushing off. She was grateful that she had worn her silk lavender dress, a birthday gift from her father and stepmother in Florida. Ordinarily she wouldn't wear anything so dressy to the office, but this morning her spirits had needed a lift—perhaps because it was a special occasion and because she was most definitely on her own and alone this year.

Opening the lounge door, a heavy French perfume assailed her senses before she spotted Giselle standing at the spacious wall mirror. She was pulling back her pale blond hair into a sleek chignon, and her amber eyes darted briefly toward Katie in the mirror before returning to her own lovely reflection.

"Hi!" Katie said. "It seems I'm going along for lunch."

"So I hear." Giselle's slight French accent put an elegant edge on the words. Her black silk suit, a designer creation, was terribly chic.

Katie rummaged in her handbag for her hairbrush, feeling awkward beside the poised woman. She had often tried to be friendly, but Giselle had always rebuffed such overtures.

"Where are we going?" she ventured.

"A surprise," Giselle answered, her eyes ignoring Katie in the mirror.

What have I done to make her dislike me? Katie puzzled. She knew that Giselle enjoyed the company of very few women, though David Wallace's late wife had been her best friend. It seemed that her life revolved around men, two of whom she had married and divorced before she was thirty.

Taking a final pleased glance at herself, Giselle turned and left the room.

"See you in a minute," Katie called after her, but the woman either didn't hear or didn't bother to answer, and the door swung shut.

Katie shrugged and ran the brush through her hair. Studying her image in the mirror, she recalled how her mother had once described her: " . . . the creamy oval face of your English great-grandmother, the dark hair of your Irish great-grandfather, and the gray-green eyes of your French and German forebears. But, most importantly, you have their fire and faith. You'll make it."

Well, her mother would be disappointed now if she happened to be looking down from heaven. Since the breakup with Stan her faith had suffered a mighty blow, and there was very little zest for life. She jammed her brush into her handbag and hurried out to the office.

Giselle and Bob stood near the enormous ficus benjamina plants by the plate-glass doors.

"Sorry to keep you waiting," Katie apologized.

"No problem," Bob answered. He held the door open as they walked out into the roar of traffic and the warm October breeze. She had the uneasy feeling that he was a little more interested in her than he ought to be.

Giselle glanced back at them curiously as she led the way to the parking lot, black high heels clicking smartly against the pavement.

Bob unlocked the front passenger door of his car, and Giselle quickly moved forward, slipping in with a flash of slim legs. He opened the back door for Katie, and she smiled up at him, content to sit behind the other woman.

As they pulled out onto Century Boulevard, Bob looked over at Giselle. "Excited about the cruise?"

She shrugged. "Not especially, although it does get me away from my desk."

Appalled, Katie couldn't help thinking how excited she would be if *she* were planning a Caribbean cruise. Ten days of luxury and adventure, the ads promised. She had accepted Bob's job offer as office manager in order to learn the travel business and eventually to become a travel agent. But, as she had told him, right now she needed a guaranteed income rather than promises of faraway places and distant commissions.

"I'm really looking forward to it," Bob said. "David and I need a better background on some of those islands."

Katie knew that as company attorney and district administrator, Bob rarely had time for travel anymore.

"Well, it's my fourth trip to some of the ports," Giselle said. "The business possibilities are what interest me now."

Katie suspected that Giselle, who owned ten percent of the company, was angling to move up in the hierarchy. She had been an early investor in Wallace-Tyler, although Bob and David were the principal owners. They had begun the first agency as a lark, and with its instant success, had opened affiliated offices throughout the West Coast. The two men were often featured in national business magazines as "the California travel tycoons."

Katie glanced out at the heavy noontime traffic, wondering why she was required for a business lunch. Perhaps, with all three of them literally at sea on a cruise, they would turn over more responsibility to her. Though she was new with the company, they had known her for several years. Ironically, Bob, David, and her ex-fiancé, Stan, had all graduated from UCLA together and often saw each other socially.

She recalled her attraction to David Wallace before she had learned that he was married and before her engagement to Stan. Then, for a while after his wife's death, Katie had suspected that the feeling was mutual. Once, at a large party, David's brown eyes had met hers across the room and held for such an intense moment that she felt as if he were looking into her soul. She knew that if she hadn't already been engaged, she might have walked right into his life. Later that night, Stan had questioned her. "What's going on between you and Wallace?"

She had attempted a reply, then finally laughed it off and changed the subject. Thereafter she had avoided David altogether, although Stan's interest in other women had not diminished. Strangely he had discarded her for a slightly younger version of Giselle—a sophisticated, hazel-eyed blonde.

Katie wondered if she should ever forgive Stan for his betrayal, for running around with other women while they were engaged. "Swinger Stan" was how she thought of him now. The bitterness that rose to choke her was almost a physical pain. Trying to forget, she asked Bob, "Where are we going?"

"It's a surprise!" he answered, turning onto the Harbor Freeway exit.

Did they know it was her birthday? Katie wondered. Maybe they were taking her out to celebrate.

Later, as they pulled into the Port of Los Angeles shipping area, the scenery took on a nautical air. Thick coils of rope swagged between weathered posts, defining the sprawling pavement into driving and parking areas. Across the water a magnificent white cruise ship was docked at the passenger terminal. Giant blue metal cranes jutted above warehouses and container ships in the distance. Overhead the gigantic green St. Thomas Vincent Bridge spanned the seaport scene and seemingly disappeared into the brilliant blue sky.

"There's part of the surprise," Bob teased as he maneuvered the car expertly into a parking space.

Katie saw the three white restaurant ships docked nearby and looked about for David Wallace. No sign of him anywhere. Surely Bob meant part of the surprise was eating on a restaurant ship.

Letting herself out of the car, she inhaled the salty air. "How lovely it is here," she said, relieved to be free of the heavy smog. Sea gulls cawed, wheeling over the channel. Here by the wind-rippled water, she might have been thousands of miles from Los Angeles. Quite suddenly she felt as if David Wallace were watching her.

"Haven't you ever been here with Stan?" Giselle asked.

Katie shook her head. It wasn't the glamorous kind of place that Stan frequented. He preferred chic city restaurants and night clubs to impress his advertising agency clients. A quiet seaside restaurant held no allure for him, although she had once talked him into going to a restaurant at Ports-of-Call Village.

Giselle waved toward the outside upper deck of the largest restaurant ship.

15

David Wallace! As he stood to greet them, Katie caught her breath, wondering if he had been watching her after all. He seemed to be smiling at her, and she mustered a timid smile in return.

The threesome passed under a sunny yellow canopy and entered the ship. Inside, gleaming brass fittings complemented the rich, dark mahogany paneling of the grand salon. Though intriguing specialty and gourmet shops lined the passageway, they disappeared like fading scenes in a film as the three made their way to the stairway where David would be waiting. Above the stairwell a French chandelier glittered, suspended from a three-deck-high skylight.

David Wallace stood at the top of the stairs, tall and rangy, probably two inches over six feet. His white teeth flashed against his deep tan, accentuating eyes the color of rich, dark chocolate. Despite her brave resolve, Katie felt slightly dizzy at the sight of him. By the time she was halfway up the stairs, she still did not have the faintest idea of what she would say.

"Happy birthday, Katie!" David said, his eyes shining.

So he did know about her birthday! "Why, thank you," she said, breathless from the admiring gaze he focused on her.

As he greeted the others, she noted the elegant cut of his gray slacks, pale blue long-sleeved shirt open at the collar, and navy blue blazer, hitched casually over his shoulder. He might have been posing for a fashion ad. Well, she was not going to be impressed! She could not risk being hurt again.

"Since our table in the dining room isn't quite ready," he said, taking her arm and guiding her through the lounge, "we can wait out on deck."

Soft music swirled around them from outdoor speakers as David escorted her across the crowded deck. She was dazed with his nearness. No other man had ever affected her so, Katie thought, as he seated her at a small table.

Bob held Giselle's chair for her, then sat down and brought out a large manila envelope from his leather portfolio, watching David as if awaiting a signal of some kind. But the other man glanced away, commenting on the cruise ship docked across the water.

Bob spoke quickly. "Giselle's just sold seventy incentive trips to Hawaii for an insurance sales contest!"

Something unspoken hung in the air. Katie sensed the tension, an undercurrent of excitement. She was certain that it had something to do with her. Yet she felt excluded from the conversation as they discussed various tour bookings. Evidently Giselle had pulled a real coup.

Giselle accepted their compliments, smoothing her hair with long, tapering fingers, magenta nail lacquer glistening. Katie was uncomfortably aware that David was watching her. How plain he must find her compared to Giselle—and even Giselle was no match for his stunning first wife, Eva. How could he ever forget Eva?

"You're very quiet for a birthday girl," David observed.

"I'm—I'm just overwhelmed," she stammered. "I've never been here before," she added, hoping to fill the awkward silence. She forced her gaze to the ship's channel where a cluster of tugboats were anchored. Nearby a red fireboat poked out of its station, much like a snail peering tentatively from its shell. Its seeming uncertainty reflected her feelings for David—and for all men in general, for that matter.

"It's one of my favorite places," he said, watching a small flotilla of sailboats. A harbor excursion vessel, packed with tourists and dwarfed by the great white liner, moved lazily through the shimmering water. "Makes me feel as if I'm sailing for faraway ports," he continued.

"It even sounds like it," she said. High above, on the St. Thomas Vincent Bridge, traffic hummed rhythmically; and there was an occasional staccato thump of a cargo container settling on the dock. A chugging tug guided an enormous coastal freighter out to sea, spreading a gentle wake to lap against crusty pilings and shoreline.

"Have you ever been on a cruise, Katie?" David asked.

She looked wistfully at the cruise ship with its strings of colorful banners waving overhead in the warm breeze. "No . . . just some family vacation trips to Yosemite and Grand Canyon when I was in grade school." She decided not to mention that her mother had been dying of cancer during her high school and college days.

"Then it's about time you saw a little more of the world," Bob said. "How would you like to go with us on the Caribbean cruise next Wednesday?"

"Me?" she asked.

He nodded.

"Why . . . I'd go in a minute! But you *are* teasing, aren't you?"

"I know it sounds preposterous, but at the last minute, the woman from our San Francisco office couldn't make it, so we have an extra ticket. You'd be a tour director like the three of us. You know that for every twenty-five passengers we book, there's a free tour director ticket. And we've booked a hundred passengers for this trip."

"But I don't know a thing about being a tour director," she protested, then realized that her honest declaration might undermine this marvelous opportunity.

"The three of us will fill you in," David reassured her. "And there's very little left to do, since our main jobs were to generate enthusiasm and coordinate the details."

"Wallace party?" the hostess interrupted.

They followed her through the lounge and into an enclosed deck area that had been transformed into a sunny yellow-and-white Victorian dining room. As the hostess paused at their table, Giselle spoke quickly. "David, do sit by me. I hardly ever see you anymore."

Katie, still stunned and disbelieving from the sudden invitation to the cruise, meekly accepted the chair Bob held for her.

"You're really not joking about the cruise?" she asked again when they were settled with large, embossed menus.

"A travel agent *never* jokes about free trips!" David said, raising a hand in mock solemnity. "Just a hint of a free trip and most people have their suitcases packed."

Can this really be happening to me? Katie wondered, barely aware of the chatter of diners and the clatter of dishes. The enticing seafood choices on the menu swam before her eyes.

"The salmon is especially good," Bob suggested.

"That sounds fine," she said, too distracted to make a decision. Perhaps she had misunderstood about the cruise, or would have to pay for part of it . . .

Bob placed the large manila envelope on the table in front of her. "Happy birthday!" he said with a grin.

David was looking over the top of his menu as she opened the envelope. Slowly she drew out a brochure. On its cover a splendid white ship sailed between verdant islands in an indigo blue sea. *Sail the Caribbean,* it invited. A ticket, attached by a paper clip, showed a receipt marked "Paid."

"I can't believe this!" she exclaimed, finding baggage tags and a packet of information about the ship—the Golden Renaissance. "I've never received such a wonderful gift!"

David and Bob smiled at her delight, but Giselle continued to study the menu.

As the waiter took their orders, Katie flipped through the pages of the brochure. There were pictures of laughing passengers engulfed in clouds of confetti, photos of luxurious swimming pools, palm-covered islands, splendid ballrooms, sumptuous spreads of gourmet foods . . .

"You'll be Giselle's roommate," Bob said. "And you'll have all weekend for shopping and packing."

"You won't need a passport, just an I.D.," David added.

"I can't begin to thank you," Katie said, still bewildered. She was aware that Giselle, sitting opposite her, had not said a word.

When their food arrived, Katie only picked at her salmon. "What sort of clothes shall I take?"

Giselle blinked at her over a forkful of salad. "Resort wear, of course."

"Of course." Katie squeezed the lemon half over her salmon. Its pungent aroma reminded her of Giselle—sour. To begin with, Katie's "resort wear" consisted of lightweight California clothing, most of which she had sewn herself.

Suddenly famished, she dug into the salmon. The tang of lemon complemented the rich flaked meat; parsley and chives added piquancy to the white sauce. Her crispy salad greens with blue cheese and tomato slices were delicious. Even the cheesy broccoli spears were delectable.

After the table was cleared, a chorus of waiters appeared, bearing a cheesecake alight with six candles. Their voices blended in a unique rendition of "Happy birthday to you!"

"Make a wish?" Bob asked.

"How could I possibly wish for anything more?" she asked.

David smiled at her and, as their eyes met, her heart turned over. *No!* she told herself. *I will make no foolish wishes about him*. The only thing she could hope was that Giselle would be a pleasant cabinmate.

Katie closed her eyes. Opening them, she blew at the

candles, but David's intense gaze diverted her. The flames above only five of the candles went out.

"One year until your wish comes true," Giselle said.

By then it would be far too late for them to be companionable cabinmates, Katie thought.

After dessert, David asked, "How about my driving the birthday girl back to the office?"

There was an awkward silence before Katie replied, "Fine." She tried not to notice the tautness around Giselle's mouth. "And thank you all for bringing me here . . ."

"It was David's idea," Bob said.

"We thought this would put you into a seagoing mood," David explained as they stood to leave. "But I believe it has done wonders for all of us."

Had inviting her on the cruise been his idea too? Of course not. Bob was her boss, and he had told her when she was interviewed that certain privileges accompanied the job.

Walking down the steps to the ship's salon, she sighed, "I'm afraid that I'll awaken from a beautiful dream."

"Let's hope not," David said. "I'm looking forward to it too."

In the parking lot, he led her through the nautical rope barriers to a bright yellow Porsche. "Is this your car?" she asked.

"Doesn't it suit me?" he answered with a rueful smile.

"It's not that at all." She shook her head, thinking that the car looked somehow familiar. But yellow Porsches were not uncommon in a city the size of Los Angeles.

As she slid in she noticed that Bob and Giselle were parked nearby. While Bob unlocked his car, Giselle's amber eyes clouded in an expression of open hostility. Was she merely being protective of her late friend's memory? Katie didn't think so.

David climbed into the car gracefully for a man so tall, and Katie suddenly felt as nervous as a girl on her first date.

He appeared to delay, allowing Bob and Giselle to pull out of the parking lot ahead of them. Turning on the car radio, he played with the dial until he found some soft music.

The song called up memories of the evening she had talked Stan into dining at a waterfront restaurant at Ports-of-Call Village. A cruise ship had sailed out of the port past the restaurant's windows. Glowing with light, the ship had resembled a magnificent floating palace. Everyone in the restaurant had stood and applauded the spectacular sight, a romantic dream come true.

Now the dream appeared to be coming true for her. Yet her mind whirled with warnings. It was not safe to trust a man as irresistible as David Wallace. Not after her experience with Stan.

CHAPTER 2

As THEY DROVE through the parking lot, Katie watched David don a pair of sunglasses. She thought that there was something about dark glasses that made people appear remote and distant, something that masked their true identity. After her breakup with Stan, she had all but lived behind her dark glasses to hide red, swollen eyes. It seemed that she could die behind them and no one would even notice.

Seeing David in the glasses, she was reminded of Stan and of the sexy, worldly image he had tried to project. Unwillingly she felt a surge of the old bitterness.

"Something wrong?" David asked.

"No. Nothing," she answered, trying to relax. She must be careful not to be so transparent. She was grateful for the music from the car radio and for the diversion as David paid the parking fee.

She wondered if she had adequately expressed her appreciation for the lunch and trip. She tried again. "The cruise is the nicest, most unbelievable birthday present I've ever had."

"It's our pleasure," David replied.

As they pulled onto the freeway, it occurred to her that perhaps she would be expected to pay for the cruise in ways she hadn't considered—that he and Bob would assume favors she did not intend to give. There were so many wild stories about cruises . . .

"I still don't understand the duties of a tour director," she said, glancing away at the bustling port with its jumble of cranes, ships, bridges, and roads.

David was busy changing lanes. "Just be your pleasant and enthusiastic self."

"Surely there's more to it than that!"

He thought for a moment. "Well, let's start with Wednesday morning at the airport. First, we'll have to herd all of our passengers to the right plane and make sure that their luggage is checked."

"Good idea!" she agreed with a nervous laugh. "Then what?"

"Not much. The Golden Renaissance personnel will meet us at the airport, check the passenger list, and ferry us by bus to the ship."

"It sounds too simple," Katie said.

David was intent on the traffic. "The only other thing I can think of is your helping at the Wallace-Tyler party that we'll be giving our passengers. But that's catered by the ship's dining room."

"What if something goes wrong . . . if one of our people becomes sick?"

"The medical staff handles emergencies," he said. "It's rare for us to be very involved once we're aboard ship."

Katie felt relieved. It sounded as if she could carry out her duties with very little effort. Still, it didn't answer the question of David's or Bob's personal expectations of her. Because of her childhood faith and her current moral code, she was a virgin, and she did not intend to sacrifice her virginity in payment for a cruise or anything else. She had promised her dying mother, and she had promised God. Perhaps she had drifted away from Him since Stan ambled into her life, but she had kept her promise of purity.

She felt David looking at her.

"There's nothing for you to worry about," he said.

She wondered if he had read her mind. Or had he heard that her unwillingness to compromise had caused the breakup with Stan? In the end, she had learned that her fiancé was running around with far less virtuous girls. Hardest to take was the fact that he blamed *her*! "You should have been named Pollyanna!" he had stormed in a moment of frustrated yearning. She would have married him in a minute, but he had always found excuses to delay, to back away from the ultimate commitment.

She wondered now whether Stan had ever intended to marry her. Perhaps she had only represented a challenge for him—a treasure beyond reach—which only further excited his imagination. She knew, too, that he considered her an asset to his business, an appropriate girl for impressing the older and more exemplary clients of his advertising agency.

As David pulled onto Century Boulevard, she noticed a carful of young women staring at them. For a moment she was perplexed, then realized that it was David they were watching. His color rose under his tan.

Did women often throw themselves at him? Katie wondered. She had never heard such rumors, although there had been nasty ones about his late wife, Eva, and the man in whose private plane she had crashed. Was David, too, accustomed to a wild lifestyle?

The girls in the adjoining lane laughed and waved, to David's further embarrassment—or pretended embarrassment. If he were a womanizer like Stan, he was probably enjoying the attention!

Back at the office David headed for the conference room where Bob, Giselle, and two of the other directors were taking their places behind the long conference table.

"See you later, Katie," he called.

"Yes . . . and thank you again!"

She sat down at her desk. Opening the top drawer, she noticed an envelope addressed to her. She recognized Bob's handwriting. Tearing open the envelope, she read the enclosed memo: "Let's not mention your trip until Tuesday afternoon. I'll put out a general memo then. Bob"

Good idea, Katie thought. No reason to stir up a rash of complaints and jealousy among the other employees, many of whom had been with the company for a much longer time. She would simply have to clear up her paperwork as inconspicuously as possible.

Smiling in anticipation, she dug in.

It was late when the quarterly meeting adjourned, but Katie was so preoccupied that she hadn't noticed the time.

"You must be one of our most dedicated employees," David remarked over her shoulder.

Startled, Katie looked around the room. Except for board members leaving the conference area, she was the only one there. "I'm trying to clear my desk," she explained.

"May I drive you home?" he asked.

"No. No, thank you," she answered quickly. "I have my own car."

He smiled. "See you at the airport on Wednesday then. I have a pile of work to finish at the downtown office too." He waved and was gone.

She sat wishing that she weren't so apprehensive, so

mistrustful of men. Surely he must think her not only absurdly naïve, but ungrateful as well.

Finally she grabbed the manila envelope with the cruise brochure, ticket and tags, and locked up her desk. In the supply room, she found maps and brochures describing the five Caribbean islands they would visit: St. Maarten, Antigua, Barbados, Martinique, and St. Thomas. She slipped the materials into the envelope for later study.

Back home in her condo, she threw herself into getting ready for the trip. Suddenly it occurred to her that she should share her exciting news with her grandmother! Gran Lucy would worry if she phoned later and there was no answer. No point in putting any more gray hairs on that dear head!

Sitting back on the pale yellow Victorian sofa that Gran Lucy had given her, Katie listened as the phone began to ring in Northern California. From the sofa, she surveyed the furnishings in the rest of her living room.

There were two light blue armchairs upholstered in floral needlepoint from Gran Lucy, along with some lamps and a charming little French iron table with painted leather inserts. The old walnut étagère in her dining area was filled with antique china, a recent birthday gift from her grandmother.

Katie cherished every piece, not only because of the sentimental value, but because each one had been crafted with such loving care. Her taste in furnishings aside, she often thought that she was a throwback to the turn-of-the-century; in the swinging city of Los Angeles, she felt like an alien from another era.

Finally Gran Lucy was on the phone wishing her a happy birthday. "I was praying for you, Katie," she said, explaining why it took her so long to answer the telephone. "You know me. Not even the telephone can interrupt my conversations with the Lord."

Katie smiled. "I should have realized how late it is, but I'm so excited. I think your prayers have been answered," she teased. "I'm leaving next week for a cruise!"

Gran Lucy seemed delighted to hear the news, but when Katie finished, she said, "It wasn't my prayers, honey. I never prayed for you to go on a cruise. What I pray for is that you will find the right man."

Katie paused, wondering if she should tell her about David.

"You still there, Katie?"

"Yes . . ."

"*Is* there a man involved in this?"

By the time she had explained how the cruise had come about, it sounded a bit strange to her too. To receive a free Caribbean cruise after only two months with the company seemed most unusual. Moreover, she had come to know these people through Stan.

"The men . . . are they married or divorced?" her grandmother asked.

"David is a widower," Katie answered. "Bob is separated."

After a long silence, Gran Lucy said, "I hear that some of the cruise ships have ministers and priests for religious services, so it must be all right." She laughed. Have a wonderful time, Katie, dear. I'll be praying for you."

Katie was still smiling when she hung up. Gran Lucy never worried long about anything; she gave it all up to the Lord in prayer. If it hadn't been for her listening love and her prayers . . .

By midnight she had planned her wardrobe, to be supplemented by the purchase of some black heels and white sandals, along with a respectable-looking suitcase and carry-on case. After studying her budget, it appeared there might still be some money left for the side tours and tipping suggested in the brochures—and even for a little shopping on the islands.

Saturday disappeared in a whirl of shopping, packing, and making the necessary arrangements to close her condo. But on Sunday morning it occurred to her that she hadn't asked anyone to care for her plants. How could she have forgotten?

She dashed down the hallway for Mrs. Sanders' door. They had met in the laundry room a year ago, shortly after Katie had moved in, and had been fast friends ever since. Something about her reminded Katie of Gran Lucy.

As Katie knocked at Mrs. Sanders' door, her elderly neighbor arrived from behind.

"Looking for me?" she asked with a delighted smile. She was wearing her Sunday best and was surely coming home from church.

"Yes. And I'm afraid that I'm looking for a favor too." She explained about the sudden trip and needing someone to water her plants.

"It's my pleasure," Mrs. Sanders said. "I know the routine, so don't worry." She gave Katie a hug. "You just have a wonderful time!"

Tuesday at lunchtime Katie bought a stunning white suit at one of the most expensive shops in the area. Mistakenly labeled a size fourteen instead of a size ten, the suit was marked down to a fourth of its summer price.

On Tuesday night there was a check in the mail for a hundred dollars from Gran Lucy. "Buy yourself something pretty," she wrote.

You've just paid for my suit, dear Gran, Katie thought happily.

It was after midnight before everything was packed in her new tan suitcase. Anticipation mounted so that she doubted she would be able to sleep at all. She laid out her new white suit and a jewel-tone turquoise blouse for the next morning. Perhaps white wasn't the smartest thing for traveling, but the suit was washable, and she had never felt so attractive in anything before.

Taking a final look around her apartment, she stopped in the kitchen for a mug of hot chocolate. Perhaps it would help her sleep.

Moments after slipping between the cool sheets, she was dreaming of David Wallace, although upon awakening she couldn't recall any of the details.

At six o'clock the next morning, Katie approached the airline reception area, her heart racing with excitement. When she saw David striding toward her, the night's dream flickered elusively.

"You look beautiful, Katie," he said, pinning a yellow Wallace-Tyler Travel and Tour badge on the lapel of her white suit. "Now it's time to earn your keep." He handed her a clipboard with a list of passengers' names. "Just send people who are wearing blue Golden Renaissance badges to Bob or to me, and check them off your list."

"Sounds simple enough."

He went on to detail the other arrangements. David and Bob would help tour group members with their tickets and luggage. Giselle was already at the departure gate to meet them with a duplicate list of tour members to be certain that no one was lost in the bustling terminal.

David reached for Katie's suitcase. "Now, if I may take your luggage, ma'am, I'll get you checked through right away."

She suppressed a giggle and waved to Bob in the distance. Moments later, excited tour group members wearing the blue badges surrounded her. She checked their names off her list and sent them on to Bob and David for further processing.

It became simple to spot the tour group members, not only by their badges, but from their beaming faces. It was as though all of them sensed that they were soon to step into another world—and were already experiencing the release of tension and daily anxiety.

Finally all one hundred passengers were accounted for and boarded, their luggage checked. Katie stepped onto the plane with David, Bob, and Giselle. Glancing at her ticket, Katie realized that, while the three of them were seated together, she had been placed far behind. She decided not to say anything to Giselle, who had evidently arranged the seating.

Katie found her row. She would just make the best of it, and proceeded by stowing her carry-on case under the seat in front of her. Still, she couldn't help but notice Giselle nestling comfortably between the two attractive men, toward the front of the plane.

An elderly couple, who introduced themselves as Ella and Edwin Goodman, sat down beside her. "It's our first cruise," Edwin said, his blue eyes sparkling. "And we mean to enjoy it."

"It's mine too," Katie confided, admiring her seatmates. Edwin was a distinguished man—tall and erect, with a silky thatch of white hair. His wife, Ella, was slim, tanned and lovely, her silver hair cropped stylishly.

"I have the impression that the two of you enjoy almost everything," Katie said.

"We do," Edwin answered, catching his wife's hand in his. "Don't we, honey?"

Ella Goodman's green eyes danced as she answered her husband. "Life's never been dull yet."

Katie pulled out her new paperback novel, but the Goodmans' animated conversation kept her entertained. Though they must have been well into their seventies, their youthful spirits belied their age. Gran Lucy would have called them "the salt of the earth."

Occasionally Katie glanced out her window. Once the city itself with its endless suburbs and smog was behind them, she marveled at the craggy foothills thrusting from the blueness of the earth. Mist lay in the valleys, rising in wraithlike wisps. Here and there the sun shimmered on lakes and rivers, transforming them into golden mirrors. Patches of white clouds floated in the blue sky. She thought that if she were to spend a lifetime flying, she would never lose the wonder of seeing the earth from high above.

"We are now flying at an altitude of 35,000 feet," the pilot announced.

Soon the mingled aromas of coffee and bacon drifted through the plane. As the pilot described the sights below, efficient flight attendants served breakfasts of fresh orange juice, cheesy omelets with bits of parsley and bright red cherry tomatoes, hot buttered English muffins, and curls of crisp bacon.

Katie sat back, relishing every bite.

Once, David passed down the aisle, smiling at her, and her pulse quickened.

"How's it going?" he asked.

"Wonderfully, just wonderfully, thank you!" she answered brightly and saw his eyes light up as if he, too, had been caught up in her excitement. After he was gone she couldn't help noticing the Goodmans exchange a curious look.

It seemed only a short time before the spicy aromas of pasta and tomato sauce greeted them, and the attendants were serving lunch.

Katie looked down at her tray. "But we've just eaten! We'll have to run around the airport ten times to work off the calories!"

Edwin chuckled. "From what we hear, we'll all be gaining a pound a day, if not more, on the cruise!"

"You're almost too thin, Katie," Ella said. "Weight is certainly not a problem for you."

Katie nodded. "Not too long ago I was nearly twenty pounds overweight." Just thinking about it caused her to forego the rolls and most of the dressing.

"Were you dieting?" Ella asked.

"No, I just couldn't eat for a while."

"There must have been a man involved," Edwin said.

She nodded. It was not as painful now recalling the last three months of her engagement to Stan, but the details were still vivid in her mind. At first she had refused to believe that he would betray her—especially not with the secretary who had the worst reputation in the entire company. Ironically it was Katie who had introduced the two of them at an office party.

When Stan's affair with the girl became obvious, Katie began to eat compulsively as if she were trying to destroy her body, or perhaps hide her old self under a layer of fat. In those three months of anguish, she had gained twenty pounds. Then, after she had returned Stan's ring and no longer had an appetite, her excess weight had melted away. A sad way to lose weight, she thought.

Edwin Goodman looked thoughtful. "There's usually a woman involved too."

"Sometimes even more than one," Katie replied bitterly.

She was grateful when they changed the subject to travel. It seemed that the Goodmans had traveled all over the United States, digging at archaeological sites and backpacking through the Rocky Mountains.

"We're getting old enough now to prefer a more leisurely pace," Edwin said.

Ella smiled. "You'll never be old."

After the flight attendant removed their trays, Katie set her watch forward to Florida time.

It seemed that she had no more than settled back to her book, a historical romance set appropriately in the Caribbean, than the plane began its descent over lush green vegetation and white sand—only a hint of the tropical splendors to come.

As the passengers disembarked into the brilliant sunshine, there were friendly Golden Renaissance tour guides to help them collect their luggage.

"Didn't I tell you they'd be here to take over?" David asked, as they were escorted to a bus. "From here on, we can sit back and enjoy the trip."

He was just behind her as she climbed onto the bus, and she was pleasantly disturbed once more by the deep rumble of his voice. He waited as Katie sat down at a window seat, then moved in beside her.

Glancing at him in profile, she noticed that a lock of dark, wavy hair had pulled loose and hung slightly over his high forehead. Her eyes wandered to his straight patrician nose, the high cheekbones and angular chin with its deep cleft, then to the full, sensuous lips. It was a strong face, but as he turned to her, there was warmth and tenderness in his expressive brown eyes.

"Excited about the cruise?" he asked.

"I've never been so excited in my life!" she replied honestly, but there was an element of suspense that troubled her.

For a moment she expected him to slide his arm around the back of her seat, but her apprehension must have been apparent. Still, he seemed pleased to be with her.

Looking out the window, Katie was barely aware of the bustle of passengers and porters hauling luggage. The heat and humidity enhanced the musky fragrance of David's aftershave.

She heard Giselle's voice and turned to see her taking a seat across the aisle. "It seems to me that you're managing very well for a novice," she said meaningfully.

Katie blushed and focused on the people boarding the bus. When Bob slid in beside Giselle, the uneasy moment passed. Either David hadn't noticed Giselle's caustic comment or had chosen to ignore it, Katie decided.

While David settled back to read through some paperwork, Katie opened the book she'd begun on the plane. But his nearness distracted her, and she was relieved when the bus neared its destination, giving her a glimpse of a startlingly beautiful ship.

"Is that our ship?" she asked.

David leaned forward to peer past the people in front of them, his arm against hers, its warmth and strength unnerving her. "That's the Golden Renaissance," he said as if their casual contact had no effect on him at all.

Everyone in the bus strained now for a better view, chattering and laughing, caught up again in the festive atmosphere.

Closer now, they could see the ship more clearly. The Golden Renaissance was as magnificent as its name, rising majestically against the blue sky. The bus braked to a stop, bringing the passengers to their feet in their eagerness to board her.

Hurrying off the bus, they were guided to a building in which they exchanged tickets for keys to their cabins. Katie looked at her large plastic key, stamped with the number of the cabin she would share with Giselle: E77. Europa Deck, Cabin 77. David was right behind with his key for E75, the adjoining cabin he would be sharing with Bob Tyler.

As they emerged into the sunshine, the ship's photographer snapped a picture of Katie and David, a life preserver bearing the name of the ship in the background. Too late, it occurred to Katie that they could easily be mistaken for a couple traveling together.

Flustered, she said for as least the third time that day, "Isn't this exciting!" Perhaps David would think her naïve, but everyone seemed infected with a spirit of enthusiastic abandon.

"The first time is always the most exciting for everything," David said, looking down at her.

Katie had the distinct impression that, if it had not been for the photographer waiting for them to move on, David might have taken her in his arms.

CHAPTER 3

KATIE WALKED UP the gangway of the great white ship, her hair flying in the balmy Florida breeze, her heart thumping with the beat of the calypso music spilling from an upper deck.

As the line of passengers in front of her came to an abrupt stop, David asked, "What do you think of her so far?"

Katie looked at the Golden Renaissance. The ship was enormous, its bow rising gracefully in a sharp curve to the many open decks above. She smiled. "I feel as if I've stepped into a living travel brochure!"

David smiled. "You're just what we need," he said. "A shot of infectious enthusiasm."

She wished that he weren't wearing his dark glasses now so that she might read the expression in his eyes.

Just behind David in line, Giselle had removed her beige suit jacket, revealing a nearly backless beige silk halter blouse. Despite the brisk breeze, every hair of her blond chignon was in place. Her eyes flickered in faint amusement. "Really, David," she said, "*a shot of infectious enthusiasm?''* Her accent added intimacy to the husky voice, as if they shared old secrets.

Katie's heart plunged at the sight of David and Giselle—the cool, beautiful blonde and the tall, darkly handsome male. They looked so right together.

If her enthusiasm had not infected her cabinmate, Katie was heartened by the exuberance of the laughing, jubilant people in the line ahead. Not even Giselle could ruin this moment. Katie wished that her hands were free to clap to the rhythms of the calypso music.

On board, crisp rows of white-jacketed attendants stood like an honor guard, their black slacks sharply creased, patent shoes gleaming. For each embarking passenger, the row moved forward in greeting. Suddenly an attendant was stepping toward her, his white-gloved hand outstretched for her cabin key and small case.

"Welcome to the Golden Renaissance," he said with a lilting Italian accent. His name tag read "Paulo." He led her into the luxurious salon.

Katie caught her breath. This was nothing like the little restaurant ship in San Pedro! This was a magnificent floating hotel, its elegant decor enhanced by elaborate crystal chandeliers and plush gold carpeting befitting a palace. Following her attendant through a maze of corridors, she realized that they had lost David, Bob, and Giselle.

The passageways and elevators were crowded with attendants ushering in new passengers. Others, who had been aboard for a short time, referred to maps of the ship as they got their bearings.

As Paulo unlocked the door to cabin E77, another white-jacketed attendant hurried past, carrying Giselle's white leather hand luggage.

"Excuse, please," he said, and placed Giselle's case on the bed by the porthole.

Katie stood open-mouthed as Paulo tried to apologize in his halting English. "Don't worry. It isn't your fault," she said. If it was that important for Giselle to have the bed by the porthole, what did it really matter?

He flashed a grateful smile, turned on the radio to soft music, then quickly showed her the cabin.

It was compact, but scrupulously clean. The attractive decor featured a gold, orange and tan Roman wall mural—a touch of ancient Rome amid the most modern of conveniences. A bowl of fruit graced the white formica coffee table. Paulo had placed her case on the twin-sized bed nearest the bath. A small dressing table and two occasional chairs left very little walking space.

"The suitcases . . . under the beds when they are unpacked," he suggested, then pointed out the life jackets in the closets which also contained hangers on top and drawers for additional storage at the bottom. The floor plan was so cleverly designed that everything could be quite comfortable—if only Giselle would be agreeable!

As Paulo closed the cabin door behind him, Katie decided to unpack her carry-on case and freshen up. At least she could learn where everything fit best. And she was eager to change from her high heels into more comfortable walking shoes.

In minutes she had decided where to store the few things she had brought with her. When she finished, she leafed through the pamphlets and brochures on the dresser. There was a ship's newspaper published daily, a deck plan, and other interesting information. It would take her a while just to learn the ropes.

She was brushing her hair when there was a knock at the door. Opening it, she found David and Bob in the corridor.

"We've come to escort you deckside," David said. "The first time out, you have to watch us sail."

"I'd love it!" she said, grabbing her key and deck plan, and putting them into her white canvas handbag.

Bob wore his usual boy-next-door grin, but David looked ill at ease for an instant before she preceded them down the narrow hallway. Behind her they laughed companionably. She knew the two of them had been friends since childhood, irrevocably bonded by a near-tragic automobile accident during high school in which both almost lost their lives.

Calypso music drifted through the air as they stepped into the sunshine. On this deck there was a shallow swimming pool for children surrounded by colorful lounge chairs. Beyond, there were two other open decks, each stretching out to the beautiful blue water far below. "It's even lovelier than I expected," she said.

"Let's go down to the Promenade Deck," Bob suggested, leading the way down the steps to the Ocean Deck, then to the enormous deck below. Here there was a large swimming pool, bright plastic chaise lounges, tables and chairs, and still plenty of room for the passengers who milled about, getting acquainted.

The calypso band played at the far end of the spacious deck. On the dock below men swarmed about, loading baggage and supplies. And on the other side was the Atlantic Ocean, its dark blue depths shimmering with the promise of adventure.

"Where's Giselle?" she asked. "She was right behind us when we boarded."

Bob chuckled. "Now that's one roommate you won't have to worry about. She probably knows the ship inside out already."

Almost too soon an announcement was issued over the loudspeaker, "All visitors ashore, please. All visitors ashore. The ship will be sailing in five minutes."

It seemed only moments before a loud blast of the ship's horn signaled that they were at last underway. The stately ship glided slowly away from the dock and into the open sea, guided by two large tugs.

As she walked around the deck with the men, Katie noticed again the openly admiring glances of women of all ages—stunned by David's good looks. She felt an odd twinge of jealousy and wondered if it had bothered Eva, his late wife. Probably not. Eva had always appeared so confident, but then she had had everything—wealth, beauty . . . and David. What else could Eva Wallace have needed to satisfy her?

"The peace of God," Gran Lucy would have said. She would have called Eva one of "the restless ones."

Watching as the tugs guided the majestic ship out of port, Katie turned to view the magnificent pink-and-gold sunset off the Florida coast.

Later, as the coastline disappeared, the refreshment bar opened near the swimming pool, and they joined the others moving toward the outdoor tables. They had been served when Giselle arrived, an exotic rum drink in hand. "I made our table arrangements with the maitre d'," she said. "Didn't any of you remember that's the first thing one does on a cruise?"

Bob laughed. "You're so well traveled, Giselle, that we knew we could leave it to you."

Giselle turned her eyes skyward in dismay. "You're incorrigible. But don't expect me to do everything for all of you." She sat down next to David and absently rested a proprietary hand on the arm of his navy blazer. There was certainly nothing absent-minded about the way she took possession of him, Katie thought. Giselle knew precisely what she was doing.

David seemed unaware of Giselle's hand on his arm. In

fact, if she didn't feel so resentful, Katie thought she might laugh at the irreproachable look on his face. Was he really so oblivious to her charms? Giselle was surely the most glamorous woman they had seen on the ship so far.

Katie glanced at her as she lit a cigarette. Giselle was one of those rare women with slim hips and a voluptuous bosom, now extremely conspicuous against her silk halter as she sat back exhaling smoke. Her bare shoulders were smoothly tanned.

"I'm still not thrilled about eating at the first sitting," Giselle pouted.

"We appreciate your giving in," Bob said. "We're unfashionable clods."

The conversation turned to their Caribbean itinerary. The first two-and-a-half days of the trip would consist of the leisurely cruise to St. Maarten, followed by four days of island hopping. That would give them another two-and-a-half days for the return trip to Florida.

"I'm glad for the rest before we begin to play tourist," Bob said. "We can spend the next two days eating."

David laughed. "Would you believe that it's only an hour before our first meal on board?" He turned to Katie. "Cruises are notorious for ruining one's figure."

Giselle stood to leave and stretched languidly. "Well, I've never gained an ounce on a cruise. As a matter of fact, I'm skipping dinner and turning in for a nap."

As Giselle strolled seductively beyond the swimming pool, a thought occurred to Katie: "How can I dress for dinner if she's sleeping?"

"No problem," David said. "We wear what we have on tonight. The luggage probably won't arrive in our cabins until after dinner."

"Tomorrow night is the Captain's Gala," Bob said. "You can dazzle us then."

"She's dazzling just the way she is," David said, his brown eyes frankly admiring.

She blushed. "Thank you," she said, glancing down at her white suit which looked amazingly crisp and fresh after a day of travel.

"Shall we give you a tour of the ship?"

Bob darted a questioning look at him.

"I'd love it," Katie said, curious about the nonverbal messages that so often passed between the two men.

The last rays of daylight lingered as the three of them started up the steps to the Ocean Deck. Here and there, lights on the ship began to glow.

"Are you game to start all the way at the top of the ship and work your way down?" David asked her.

"I'm game," she replied. "We've been sitting all day and I can use the exercise." From her handbag, she produced the deck plan to follow as they explored the ship.

After climbing the three flights of stairs to the top of the ship, she was surprised to find that the Sun Deck was not much more than an enormous wooden platform surrounding the stack from which huge clouds of smoke billowed, huffing and hissing, into the near darkness. A small building near the stack housed exercise equipment and mats. Otherwise there was only the railing around the deck, the ocean far below, and a sky sparkling with stars.

For a long time she stood lost in the symphony of night sounds at sea. After a while she turned to look at David. He stood some distance from her, studying the sky. His head was turned away, but he was so still that he might have been praying.

"David's something of an amateur astronomer," Bob said.

Katie was only half listening. "Astrologer?"

"No, *astronomer*," Bob corrected. "He won't have a thing to do with astrology."

Katie breathed a quiet sigh of relief. Gran Lucy loved what she called stargazing herself, but was adamant in her distaste for astrology. "The Bible strictly forbids it," she had often said.

"David has a good-size telescope at his apartment," Bob said.

"Really?" How little she knew about him. She knew little, too, about stars, except where to find the Milky Way . . . and something about Venus, the evening star. Locating it now, she recalled that it was known as the wishing star, referred to by the poets as "love's harbinger." She quickly turned away, wanting nothing to do with a messenger of love.

Later, as they made their way down into the ship deck by deck, Bob excused himself at the purser's office. Katie and David continued their exploration, looking in on the library where a few people were already busily writing post cards. Farther down, there were boutiques, a gift shop and a perfume shop, all now closed.

"They'll be open later," David said, noticing her wistful expression.

"I doubt that I'll be buying much anyway," she said, then wished that her comment hadn't sounded so negative. It was the gift of a lifetime merely to be a passenger on this cruise.

David seemed to enjoy playing tour guide, she thought, as they took an elevator to the cinema at the bottom of the ship. It was dark and quiet, and as they stepped into the empty theater, their hands accidentally brushed.

"Sorry," he said quickly, but he didn't look sorry at all. His brown eyes filled with longing, and she thought that he must feel as unnerved as she.

"Katie. . . ?"

"Yes?"

"How about the movie after dinner?"

Katie suddenly felt shy, remembering the electric touch of his hand. But she found herself saying, "I'd like that." The words spilled out quickly, instinctively. Reproaching herself, she wished she had said *I'd like to think about it* . . . or, *Maybe I'll unpack after dinner* . . . or any one of a thousand other excuses!

Bells chimed over the loudspeakers. "Ladies and gentlemen, dinner is now served for those at the first seating. May I wish you a *bon appetito*."

David chuckled. "After a while those bells condition everyone to drool like Pavlov's dogs, hungry or not."

She wondered if the flash of his smile conditioned women in the same way. As he guided her to the elevator, she was furious with herself for being so attracted to him.

She could think of nothing to say as the elevator doors closed behind them. She wondered what David was thinking. That she would be another easy conquest? The elevator stopped at the next deck, quickly filling with passengers on their way to dinner.

At the dining room entrance, the maitre d' appeared to escort them through the festive room. Colorful flags hung from the ceiling, and, below, a sea of tables were beautifully set with white damask cloths and tall, silver vases of red carnations. An air of expectancy filled the room as diners settled at the round tables, attended by an array of captains, waiters, and busboys.

As the maitre d' seated her with a flourish, Katie was delighted to see Edwin and Ella Goodman at their table.

"Katie! What a pleasure!" Edwin said.

"We feel that you're already a dear friend," Ella added, smiling in delight.

Bob Tyler rose from his chair and introduced the young honeymooners across the table, Marcie and Mark Bowden, and a middle-aged couple, Walt and Sondra Zelt, whose slurred response was apparently due to the rum drinks they had carried in with them from the bar.

The waiter, elegant in black suit and tie, presented huge embossed menus, and Katie puzzled over the selections— oysters, caviar, shrimp, lobster, steak, prime rib, fish, roast and other delicacies.

The busboy filled their goblets with tinkling ice water, then brought a tray of freshly baked rolls whose mouth-watering aroma had preceded him.

There was too much to choose from, Katie thought hopelessly. When she finally decided on the caviar hors d'oeuvre and prime rib for the entrée, she was surprised to find that David had made the same selections.

"You're not newlyweds, too, are you?" Edwin Goodman asked.

Katie felt her face burning. "Oh, no! We're just friends," and hurriedly explained that her cabinmate was resting.

After the conversation shifted, Edwin leaned over to apologize. "I'm so sorry. I didn't mean to embarrass you. It's just that you . . . you seem to belong together."

"Men!" Ella Goodman said, although with such an adoring look that it was obvious how she felt about her husband.

Edwin shook his head, turning to his wife. "You know *me*. If there's any possible way to put my foot in my mouth, I'll find it," he said, and they laughed congenially.

"Did I miss something?" David asked.

"Not at all," Katie replied, wishing that her blushes didn't betray her so. She would have to get a good tan—or even a burn—if she were going to continue to react like a teenager!

"You're very beautiful, Katie," David said softly, "especially when you blush."

"Never mind!" she protested with a helpless laugh. For an instant she thought that David was going to add something, but the waiter arrived just at that moment with their first course.

"It looks delicious," she said, concentrating her full attention on the tiny silver tubs of red and black caviar served with toast tips, sprigs of watercress, and slices of lemon. "I've only had caviar once before in my life . . ." She paused, remembering that it had been with Stan.

The conversation at their table turned to travel, and Katie could only listen, spellbound. With all the talk of exotic places and people, there was no question in her mind that she wanted to be a travel agent. How thrilling it would be to travel all over the world.

"It must be a lovely thought you're thinking," Ella Goodman said, speaking across her husband to Katie. "What is that quotation . . . 'If, instead of a gem or even a flower, we could cast the gift of a lovely thought into the heart of a friend . . .'"

". . . that would be giving as the angels give,'" David completed the sentence.

Katie turned to him. "You know poetry?"

"Only a little," he protested. "My mother wrote poetry and encouraged my sister and me to memorize passages. Comes in handy sometimes."

The waiter stopped to pour a glass of complimentary wine, but she waved him away. She had begun to drink while dating Stan and wanting so desperately to fit in with his crowd, but she did not intend to continue the practice. She recalled Gran Lucy saying, "Drinking is not only the devil's way into a person, but a person's way to the devil!" And Gran Lucy was usually right.

It was at dinner that Bob Tyler mentioned the heavy pitching of the ship. "I've been on many a cruise," he said, "but this is the worst pitching I've ever felt. It should smooth out when we're in the Caribbean."

"I hope so," moaned Sondra Zelt, although it wasn't clear what was causing her distress—the rum drinks topped by the bottle of wine they had nearly finished, or the movement of the ship. Her husband seemed unaware of her discomfort, intent on playfully harassing the newlywed Bowdens.

Katie finished her prime rib, green beans and potato puffs, grateful that the rolling of the ship hadn't affected her enjoyment of the delicious meal.

"Save room for dessert," Bob warned, to a chorus of groans.

After the entrées, the waiter served a selection of cakes, pies, petits fours and elegant little tarts, followed by an assortment of European cheeses and fresh fruit.

As they pushed away from the table, she half-hoped that David might forget about the movie or change his mind. But as he helped her from her chair, he said, "It's supposed to be a good movie; they only show first runs."

The elevators were crowded, so she and David made their way down the stairwells, struggling to maintain their balance against the pitching of the ship. Katie found herself wondering about his family, particularly his mother. His father's large accounting firm prepared the final accounts for Wallace-Tyler, but she knew nothing more about the Wallaces.

"What is your mother like?" she asked.

David's face clouded. "She passed away this year."

"I'm so sorry," Katie said. "Forgive me, David."

He smiled. "It's all right. You couldn't have known. I like to remember her. She was quite a lady." He was silent for a while as they continued down the stairs. "Now that I think of it, she was a lot like you, Katie. Enthusiastic, interested in others, though she didn't blush nearly as often."

Normally, neither did *she,* Katie thought as the ship lurched, throwing her against David. She looked up at him as he steadied her, thinking that he seemed inordinately pleased. Then they were both laughing as he released her.

"Here, hang on," he said, taking her hand and tucking it into his arm. She couldn't very graciously pull it away, she decided as they walked into the lighted cinema.

Inside, they found seats near the back. As they sat down she removed her hand from his arm, but he caught it back and impulsively kissed her fingertips.

"David!" she protested, pulling her hand from his.

She moved her hands well away from him when the movie began, wondering what to expect next. Was he another Stan? After all, David had been part of the same party scene when he was married to Eva. Even after her death, he had appeared at the parties for a while before dropping out to concentrate on his business.

She forced her attention to the movie, although it was nearly impossible to forget the tall man at her side.

Later, when the movie was over and the lights came on, he said, "Bob's holding seats for us in the Antilles Lounge for the First-Night-Out Party."

Katie had to think for a moment before she remembered that there was a party scheduled there.

In the lounge Bob waved at them across the crowd. He was sitting with a young woman whom she recognized as a member of the Wallace-Tyler group, but he didn't look terribly interested in her. Katie wondered if he were still in love with his wife, Suzanne, a red-headed model who had become consumed with advancing her career. No one at work seemed to know if they were merely separated or if they had actually filed for divorce.

"Thank goodness, you saved seats," Katie said to Bob. Though the room was large, people were already standing against the walls. She sank down gratefully on the small love seat, David's arm resting on the back of it behind her. She fought the impulse to relax against him. *Remember,* she cautioned herself, *you've been hurt once. Don't trust him . . . don't trust him . . .*

Staff introductions were made from the front of the lounge, then the young cruise director took over, starting "fun, games, and prizes," as he called it.

"It reminds me of those television game shows," Katie laughed as cabin numbers were called out and prizes awarded to the occupants.

Moments later, the cruise director called, "Europa 77."

"That's my number!" she said, getting up and hurrying forward. She was halfway to the front before she realized that Giselle might be coming forward to claim the prize. Glancing around, she saw no sign of her.

The cruise director was waiting to introduce her to the audience, part of the ship's get-acquainted campaign. "Katie Thompson," he said. "Where are you from, Katie?"

"Santa Monica, California," she said and thanked him for the package.

Returning to the table, she unwrapped her gift—a bottle of cologne. "And I didn't bring any perfume," she said, delightedly spraying her wrists.

After a moment David took her hand to sniff the fragrance. "It's not soft enough for you," he said. "You should smell like flowers."

She withdrew her hand and sat back. Was he so knowledgeable about women that he could match the perfume to the individual? Perhaps he'd learned from Eva who, like Giselle, made it a point to be informed about such things.

Not that there was anything wrong with that, but she had never had the money to afford many luxury items. Besides, there were more important things in life.

At midnight they wandered into the dimly lit Calypso Lounge to hear the ship's orchestra, and Katie spotted Giselle dancing with one of the ship's officers. Her sensational silvery, low-backed dress set off her blond beauty to perfection. She might have stepped from the pages of an haute-couture magazine. Over the shoulder of her dancing partner, Giselle acknowledged their entrance with the lift of a speculative eyebrow.

"It's too smoky in here," David said. "How about some fresh air?"

"Fine," she said, wondering if their hasty exit had something to do with Giselle's presence.

They wandered out to the deck and leaned on the polished mahogany railing, looking out into the night.

"Bob tells me that you know all about astronomy," she said, gazing up at the velvety sky. The brilliant stars suspended above in the darkness seemed to be keeping watch over the sleeping earth.

"Certainly not everything," David laughed. "I suppose I'll always feel like a beginner, but I do enjoy the hobby."

A line of poetry flashed through Katie's mind. "Ye stars, that are the poetry of heaven . . ."

"Byron," he responded instantly.

"You *do* know poetry!" She tried to recall some other lines: "Silent, one by one, in the infinite meadows of heaven, blossomed the lovely stars . . . the forget-me-nots of angels."

"Longfellow, I think," he said with a grin.

She looked at him in amazement, this man who knew about stars and poetry. "You continue to surprise me," she said softly.

His arm moved around her, slowly turning her toward him.

No, David, she thought, as she appealed wordlessly, but then it was too late to think. His lips touched hers tentatively and, instead of pulling away, she tilted her head and leaned forward. His mouth, warm on her lips, was gentle at first, then grew demanding, possessive, sending tremors through her as though there had never been another kiss on earth.

When they finally parted, her breath was as ragged as his; her knees, so weak that she had to grip the mahogany railing for support.

"I'm sorry," he said abruptly. "I didn't mean to do that."

She was too stunned to answer. For a long time they stood at the railing and stared out at the night sky. She must get away to sort out her thoughts.

"It's been a busy day," she finally said, "and I still have to unpack. Perhaps I'd better get back to the cabin."

"Of course," he said.

She noticed that he limped slightly as they pressed against the wind and recalled the accident that had almost claimed his life.

Outside her cabin door, she feared that he might try to kiss her again, but he asked only if he might take her to breakfast.

She unlocked the door, thinking that she had never been invited to breakfast by a man, but then she had never been on a cruise either. "Yes, thank you," she said, swallowing with difficulty. She was grateful that Giselle was not yet in the room.

As Katie began to close the door between them, she said softly, "Good night, David."

"'Night, Katie." He smiled. "See you in the morning."

She closed the door and leaned back against it, her eyes

shut. What was she feeling? Was it the first stirrings of love or only the magic of a starlit night at sea? It was a long time before she opened her eyes. Her reverie was broken by the memory of his words spoken with regret: "I'm sorry. I didn't mean to do that."

What had he meant? The words had stung like a slap. Why kiss and then apologize?!

Finding her suitcase key, Katie unpacked quickly. On her pillow was the program for tomorrow, every hour charted for anyone who cared to try to follow the scheduled events. But she could barely concentrate and placed it aside as she slipped into bed.

She tried to empty her mind, but there was too much that clamored for remembrance. As she drifted off into sleep, her last thought was of David holding her in the moonlight, his lips moving toward hers . . .

CHAPTER 4

THE MORNING LIGHT streamed in through the porthole, awakening Katie with the memory of David's kiss. She glanced at her wrist watch. She would have to hurry to be ready for the first breakfast seating at seven-thirty. She slipped out of bed, grateful that Giselle was still asleep.

Since she planned to lie in the sun after breakfast, she chose a white, blue, and green wrap-around skirt and a scooped-neck white blouse, which could be worn over her blue bathing suit. Her new white sandals completed the outfit.

She dressed quietly and was hurrying to the cabin door when Giselle rolled over, opened an eye, and said, "Don't get too involved with David. You're not his type. You'll only get hurt."

Katie stopped, staring in amazement.

"What do you mean?" she asked.

"I was one of his wife's best friends," Giselle said. "Eva and I were classmates in Switzerland. I was the maid of honor at their wedding. I *know* David Wallace."

"But . . ." Katie was taken aback. What she did was none of Giselle's concern.

"Eva was educated at the best schools. She was well-traveled and knew all the right people when David started his business," Giselle continued. "That's the kind of woman who appeals to him on a long-term basis." She rolled back to the wall, pulling the covers over her bare shoulder.

"Someone like you?" Katie asked, slightly indignant.

Giselle shrugged. "Perhaps."

Katie flared angrily. "And why are you telling me this?"

"Because I don't want to spend the last half of our trip listening to the wailing of a broken-hearted innocent," Giselle answered evenly. "Quite frankly, I find broken hearts foolish and boring."

You ought to know! Katie wanted to say, but managed to hold her tongue. A soft knock at the door deflected Katie's anger. Giselle mumbled instructions: "I have an eleven o'clock appointment with the masseuse, then another with the hairdresser. Tell David and Bob that I won't be available to help with Ports-of-Call information."

Katie grabbed her white canvas handbag and slipped out, quickly closing the door behind her, not daring to meet David's eyes.

"What's wrong?" he asked.

She forced a bright smile. "Nothing. Nothing at all." She was certain that Giselle was mistaken about David.

"You're sure?"

"Of course." She didn't like to lie, but how could she possibly tell him what Giselle had said? If Giselle loved David and wanted him for herself, she certainly had a strange way of showing it.

"Did you sleep well?" he asked.

"Like a baby! I think it was a combination of fatigue and

this marvelous sea air!" She kept up the cheerful chatter all the way to the dining room. She was determined that David should not suspect anything about Giselle's warning, but as he glanced at her, Katie wondered if she had fooled him after all.

This morning, with the draperies pulled away from the wide windows, the dining room seemed less formal. There was a magnificent view of the ocean as the ship sliced through rolling swells. At their table, Bob Tyler and Edwin Goodman rose slightly as Katie was seated.

Ella Goodman smiled brightly. "We five must be the only early birds at our table."

"Seems a shame to sleep away the whole morning," Edwin said.

"Good morning, *signorina*," the waiter said, presenting her with a breakfast menu.

Over breakfast they discussed the morning's activities. There was an exercise class as well as a walk-a-mile on the Promenade Deck. In addition, there was a ship tour, dance class, bridge class, bingo tournament, and a ten-thirty briefing on the approaching ports-of-call.

"And that's only this morning," Edwin said. He showed Katie the activities for the afternoon listed in the ship's newspaper.

"It's better to take a half-day at a time," David chuckled. "Otherwise it takes the vacation right out of the trip."

She recalled Giselle's message. "I nearly forgot. I'm to tell you that Giselle has appointments with the masseuse and the hairdresser. She won't be able to help with Ports-of-Call suggestions for our group."

David and Bob exchanged exasperated glances, but said nothing.

"Maybe I can help," Katie offered.

"Maybe," David said. He smiled so warmly that her

spirits lifted. "We'll have to go to the Ports-of-Call talk. It's only a matter of our being around the purser's office later in case our tour people have questions."

"Then I'll be there," she said, anxious to repay them for this wonderful trip.

Bob said, "Giselle's the only one of us who is really knowledgeable about these island tours." He shrugged. "I guess we'll just have to use the travel agent's rule-of-thumb—put the swingers on the booze cruises and everyone else on land tours."

"If Katie's around to smile, everything will be fine!" David said.

She felt a blush rising to her face again, then everyone laughed good-naturedly. It would be a good day in spite of its unfortunate beginning.

As they lingered over breakfast, David asked, "What would you like to do this morning?"

She wrinkled her brow in thought. "Walk-a-mile, then be lazy in the sunshine by the pool . . . and attend the Ports-of-Call talk, of course."

"May I join you for the sunshine by the pool?" he asked.

She began to respond breezily, but when she found herself looking into the soft depths of his eyes, she could only nod. It seemed as if other people in the dining room had faded away and only the two of them existed. Remembering their moonlight kiss, Katie also recalled David's puzzling words: "I didn't mean to do that."

Stepping out on the Promenade Deck into the dazzling sunshine with David, she walked quickly to the railing and stared out across the inky-blue Atlantic, whipping up frothy whitecaps as rapidly as her mind was churning her tumbling emotions. In one sense, Giselle had been right: broken hearts were foolish. All of the passions of life—the agony and the ecstasy—wrung out a heart until living was unbearable. It was wonderful to be in love, but torment when it ended. Vowing never to be vulnerable to such anguish again, she clenched her hands until her fingernails dug into her palms.

For a long time she and David stood at the railing looking out at the ocean, lost in their own thoughts. Without warning, he tipped her chin and kissed her gently on the mouth. "I'm so glad you're here, Katie," he said.

She could only stare at him, disarmed by his tenderness, but more confused than ever. Giselle's warning sounded in her brain: *Don't get involved with David . . . You'll only get hurt.*

A crowd of energetic walkers bore down on them, led by an athletic young woman, undoubtedly the exercise instructor. "Step it up! Step it up!" she called cheerily.

"It's the walk-a-mile!" Katie said and, to avoid further confrontation, dashed off to join them. "See you later!" she called back over her shoulder, then saw the hurt and surprise on David's face. At least this time she hadn't given him the opportunity to say that he hadn't meant to kiss her!

By the time they had circled back, David was gone. It wasn't until the last turn around the deck that she saw him again. He had changed into bathing trunks and was settling on a lounge chair in the crowd of sunbathers near the pool. He tried to catch her eye, but she pretended not to notice. She moved on, even when the other walkers disbanded near him. She still didn't know why she was running, only that she had to get away from him.

Stopping in the Mediterranean Lounge to catch her breath, she found herself in the spot where she and David had lingered for a few minutes during their tour of the ship. They had stayed to listen to the mellow sounds of a jazz trombonist and planned to return on future evenings. Now, she felt ashamed. She had run out on David quite rudely. It wasn't as if she had resisted his kisses. The problem was that she hadn't resisted at all! She was frightened—not so much of David—but of her growing infatuation with him.

She turned her attention to the far end of the room where a blonde hostess explained the dress code aboard ship to a group of passengers. "For evening attire, 'formal' means tuxedo or dark suit for men, and long or short evening dresses for women," she said. "'Informal' means business suit or sport jacket and slacks; for ladies, a dress, pants suit or sports outfit. 'Casual' suggests an open shirt and slacks, and skirt and blouse, or cotton dress."

Models wandered among the crowd, pirouetting gracefully to display the designer clothing that could be purchased from the ship's boutique.

"I thought that was you, Katie," Bob said, dropping to the couch beside her. "David said you'd disappeared."

"Sorry," she said, feeling a pang of guilt. "It's just that . . . I needed to get away by myself for a while." It wasn't entirely untrue, she thought.

Bob sat back with a sigh. "I need to simmer down myself." He glanced at his watch. "Unfortunately we ought to head for the Ports-of-Call talk in a few minutes or we'll have to stand through it all." He looked tired and a bit sad.

Did the models remind him of Suzanne? Katie mused. Bob had been married such a short time; it was dreadful that it seemed to be ending so soon.

Later, when she and Bob found seats in the Antilles Lounge, she saw David approaching. He had changed back into his white resort suit. His brow was furrowed, his eyes dull and flat. "Am I welcome here?"

She scooted over quickly. "Of course, David. I'm sorry to have run out on you . . ."

He didn't seem interested in hearing her explanation as he sat down, glancing around the room.

He has a temper too, she thought, reminded of Stan. Or was it that David was merely looking for someone else? Giselle?

At the front of the room, the cruise director tapped on the microphone, and the drone of the crowd subsided as they settled back to hear about island excursions, shopping tips, and the latest U. S. Customs information.

Katie noticed that David was careful not to sit too close. Why had she been so rude to him? Why had she run? Her eyes met his for an instant, finding them cold and lifeless. He continued to scrutinize Katie and Bob. Did he suspect there might be something going on between them?

Her guilt and David's quiet anger hung in the air as tangibly as if a curtain had dropped. As difficult as it was to concentrate, Katie managed to take copious notes. On St. Maarten, there were two tours—a land trip and a catamaran cruise past both the Dutch and French sides of the island; on Antigua, three tours; on Barbados, one; Martinique, two. St. Thomas offered five tours.

There was also much to learn about shopping on the islands. Although she would not be spending much money, she should be ready to answer the questions of the more prosperous passengers.

After the talk, people started for the purser's office to buy their island tour tickets. "With my notes," Katie offered, "I should be able to help a little."

"It won't be necessary," David answered coldly.

She stared at him in dismay, recalling his words at breakfast: "If Katie's around to smile, everything will be fine!"

She wanted to slink away, but she had to buy her own excursion tickets. Heartsick, she tried to study the Ports-of-Call sheet as she drifted with the crowd to the purser's office. Long lines had already formed.

As she checked off her final tour decisions, she noticed David moving among the lines of passengers to answer questions, then stopping at the purser's desk.

The tours were far more expensive than she had dreamed, and she realized she would have to use nearly all of her money. Perhaps she could skip a tour or two and stay on the ship those days.

"This is for you," David said, shoving an envelope at her. "If you don't like the selection, work it out with the purser." He quickly moved away into the crowd.

Opening the envelope, Katie discovered tour tickets for all of the islands. Wallace-Tyler had paid for them. Or maybe even David himself. She gave up her place in line and tried to catch him.

"David!" she called after him. "I can't accept this."

"Why not?" he asked angrily. "It's part of your free package as a tour director."

As he turned away, she reached out, touching his arm. "Please let me explain."

His brown eyes, flat and glittering now, met hers. "You're on!"

Nearby, people glanced at them curiously.

"Please . . . not here . . ."

"Where then?" he asked.

People all around had interrupted their own conversations to listen. She had no idea that David was the sort of man who would humiliate her publicly. He'd been so thoughtful, so gentle. She couldn't understand this steely side of him. She rushed blindly to the elevator, both hoping and fearing that he might follow—but she was alone.

Stepping out on the Promenade Deck, she walked to the port side. Now she had achieved exactly what she had been seeking all day—time to think.

Please, God, help me! Please help me to understand what

is happening to me—and to David. Taking a deep breath, Katie realized that this was the first time she had prayed in a very long time.

Looking out at the constancy of ocean and sky, she finally felt a peace stealing over her. She sat down to reconstruct the events that had prompted this miserable cold war: First, she had run from David; then, he had seen her with Bob . . . Of course! If Eva had been unfaithful as rumored, David would be especially sensitive and would have reason to be suspicious. Quite likely that was why he had been so distant when he found her sitting with Bob.

The loudspeaker crackled. "Ladies and gentlemen, luncheon is now served for the first seating . . ."

She was not at all hungry. Just the thought of food made her ill. She opened the envelope that David had given her and glanced at the excursion tickets, discovering that they matched those she had checked off on her sheet: St. Maarten's "Under Two Flags Island," Antigua's "Lord Nelson's Dockyard and Countryside," Barbados' "Island and Countryside," Martinique's "City of St. Pierre Tour," and St. Thomas's "Coral World Island Tour."

Surely David had chosen the tours for her. But how had he guessed her preferences?

Passengers carried trays of food along the port side now, no doubt from the outdoor buffet, and the tables in front of her were already taken.

"Are these chairs available?" an elderly woman asked.

"Yes," Katie said. "I was just leaving."

Giselle would probably still be with the masseuse or hairdresser. Now was the time to pick up her paperback novel.

In the corridor she was thankful that David and Bob were not in sight. When she unlocked the cabin door, she was relieved that Giselle was out too. The beds were neatly made, the dresser and table dusted, and the bathroom sparkling. She hung her blouse and skirt, and still in her blue bathing suit, slipped into the blue, green and white cover-up she had sewn from the same fabric as her skirt.

Grabbing her sunglasses and handbag, she hurried to the outside deck, jammed with passengers who had decided to eat their lunch in the sunshine.

"Looking for a lounge, Katie?" a cheerful voice called out from across the sea of sunbathers. It was Ella Goodman, who had at her side what was probably the only empty chair on the entire deck.

Katie waved, trying to smile. "Thanks! I'm coming!" She made her way through the maze of people. Someone ahead of her was heading for the lounge, but diminutive Ella was not to be talked out of it. She and Edwin seemed delighted to see her.

"Aren't you eating lunch?" Edwin asked.

"I'm not hungry," Katie answered, "I just wanted some sun."

"Where's David?" he asked.

Katie looked away. "I don't know. Maybe in the dining room."

"Why, he's right across the far corner of the pool . . ." Edwin said, then looked embarrassed as if he realized too late that he had again spoken hastily.

"You two aren't fighting, are you?" Ella asked with concern.

"We're only friends," Katie said lightly, darting a look at David, who was surrounded by a group of bikini-clad young women. One pretty brunette, in particular, seemed to have captured his attention.

"Looked to me like a lot more than that last night," Edwin remarked, despite Ella's warning frown.

Katie removed her beach cover-up and lay back, closing

her eyes, trying to relax and let the salty air and sunshine work its soothing magic.

Strange. She hadn't felt this uptight before the cruise. Cruises were supposed to be so relaxing; instead, her body felt tense. She tried to sleep, but she couldn't halt the troubled thoughts racing through her head.

"Katie, they're going to close up the buffet," Ella said. "Why don't you have some salad? You have to eat something."

"Maybe I should." Across the pool, David appeared to be having a fine time with the girls. Perhaps it was silly, but she didn't want to walk past him on the way to the buffet.

Ella, perceiving Katie's dilemma, was already up. "Let me get something for you. I want a fresh glass of iced tea anyway."

"Well, maybe just some salad and iced tea . . ."

When Ella brought her lunch on a bright yellow tray, Katie took it gratefully. "Thank you, Ella. You're a wonderful friend."

"My pleasure, dear."

She could only pick at the tossed salad and creamy cole slaw, but she drank the strong, icy tea. Feeling David's eyes on her, her hand trembled and she set the glass down quickly.

Later, the loudspeaker announced an informal champagne party for singles in the Caribbean Lounge, and many of the younger passengers got up from the chaises.

"Why don't you go?" Ella asked. "It might be fun."

"I tried being a swinging single for a while," Katie said. "I'm not much good at it."

"You're the prettiest girl on the ship," Edwin said with great conviction, then smiled at his wife. "Except for Ella, of course."

Katie smiled. "And you two are the kindest couple," she said.

When she looked for David, she saw that he had left. Feeling heartsick, she tried to settle down with her book, but her eyes moved absently over the pages. What had she done? Why had she been so willful and foolish? Perhaps if he hadn't pressed her so hard . . .

"I've had enough sun," Katie said to the Goodmans as she slipped into her cover-up. "I'll see you both later."

"You won't recognize us tonight at the Captain's Gala," Edwin said with a grin.

The Captain's Gala! She had forgotten all about the formal evening. And she had planned to wear a filmy green gown with her silver bag and high-heeled sandals. Well, she would just skip the whole affair and ask for a tray to be sent to her room, or sneak down to the grill for a slice of pizza.

After a refreshing shower, she strolled out onto the Europa Deck. There were few passengers here, and the children who usually splashed happily in the shallow pool were probably down for afternoon naps. Katie basked in the quiet, feeling the tension draining from her.

"Katie?"

Preoccupied, she heard his voice which seemed to be coming from far away. It took her a moment to realize that David was standing beside her.

"I'm sorry," he said. "I hope you'll forgive me." He handed her a small gift-wrapped package.

Katie accepted it reluctantly and closed her eyes. "Really, David, a present isn't necessary. Besides, it was *my* fault."

Smiling hesitantly, he perched on an adjoining lounge. "I'd like us to be friends again," he said, his eyes hopeful.

How could she ever explain? "I'm sorry I ran from you this morning . . ." She looked down. "I needed to be alone."

"I think I understand," he said.

They looked at each other for a long moment, weighing each other carefully.

"Open the package," he urged.

She tore away the exquisite gold paper and, seeing the contents, gasped. "It's Joy—Patou's Joy," she whispered. She knew only that it was one of the most expensive perfumes in the world. "Oh, David . . ."

She opened the bottle carefully, and the subtle flowery scent issued from it like the essence of a summer garden. "It's lovely, but you shouldn't have . . ."

"You're lovely," he said huskily.

She hesitated for an instant, then daubed a drop behind each ear, leaning toward him so he could catch a whiff. He bent down, and the fragrance enfolded them, weaving its spell. He moved away reluctantly.

"It's just right for you," he said, and paused. "Friends again?"

"Of course, David . . . and thank you."

"May I come by for you about six—that is, if you would allow me to escort the most beautiful girl on the ship to the Captain's Gala."

She nodded, trying to hide her happiness and the quick tears that had sprung to her eyes.

At the aft door, he flashed a careful smile, and she felt a momentary pang. Had he meant *exactly* what he had said? That now they were merely friends?

CHAPTER 5

THE FRAGRANCE OF JOY and the memory of David's parting smile lingered as Katie dressed for the Captain's Gala. Between Giselle's withering glances and thoughts of David, it was an effort to settle down at the dressing table.

Katie studied her reflection in the mirror. She had held up very well despite the day's torment. Her sparkling eyes were now nearly as sea green as the filmy dress that lay on her bed, her face, lightly tanned from the afternoon sun.

"Who gave you the perfume?" Giselle asked as she pulled several expensive dresses from her closet to make her selection for the evening.

"A friend." Katie's answer was noncommittal.

"Was it our dear David?"

Katie didn't reply and reached for her hairbrush.

"He's been known to be extravagant. Just don't come crying to me when he disappoints you."

Katie pretended not to have heard. There was no appropriate response, anyway. Brushing back her hair, she decided on a simple style. With Giselle's barbed comments so expertly aimed, Katie wanted only to escape the cabin as quickly as possible. She was grateful when her roommate headed for the shower.

Katie slipped into her evening gown, strapped on silver high-heeled sandals, and peered into the mirror. Her dark hair swung freely over one shoulder, and was brushed sleekly back behind the other. The sea green dress with its scooped neck, tiny sleeves, and skirt falling into subtle petals was enchanting. For once, she looked exactly as she had hoped she might.

"See you later, Giselle!" she called out.

Closing the cabin door behind her, Katie felt relieved to have evaded her roommate's scrutiny. Her ensemble certainly wouldn't be Giselle's idea of high fashion.

Standing in the corridor, Katie wondered what to do next. David wasn't due for another fifteen minutes. Down the hallway she noticed a young woman helping two children tape pictures to the walls. Of course! The youth rooms were just off the children's pool. The morning newspaper had invited passengers to view the children's artwork there.

As Katie approached, the youngsters gazed at her with undisguised admiration. Blue-eyed blonds with cherubic faces, they appeared to be sister and brother—the girl, about five years of age; the boy, perhaps four.

"You look like a princess," the girl said, her blue eyes wide.

Katie laughed. "Thank you. You're pretty enough to be a princess yourself."

The boy placed a small plump hand in Katie's. "Come look at *my* pictures."

The girl reached for Katie's other hand.

Their small, soft hands in hers, Katie glanced down the corridor to be certain that David wouldn't miss her here. "I'd love to," she answered.

Praising their drawings of ships at sea and islands with palm trees, she couldn't help hoping that David liked children. One of her greatest disappointments with Stan had been his attitude toward children, a home, and marriage. "You're crazy, Katie," he had said. "It's almost the year two thousand! Who wants to be saddled with kids and mortgages nowadays?"

Saddened, she couldn't imagine David wanting that either. After all, he was a wealthy businessman whose life had always revolved around travel. He hadn't had children with his first wife. Why should he want them now?

She realized how far her thoughts had wandered and turned her attention to the children's artwork. Minutes later she looked up to see David striding toward her, breathtaking in his midnight blue tuxedo.

"She's our princess," the little girl piped out as he approached.

The boy leaned far back to look up at David. "But *he* looks like the prince."

They laughed and David patted the child's shoulder. "Sorry, but I'm going to have to carry your princess away."

"Are you *really* going to carry her?" the boy asked.

David raised an amused eyebrow and grinned.

"We have to go now, but we'll see you again," Katie reassured the children.

As she and David walked down the corridor, he said, "That boy was right. You *do* look like a princess."

"I feel like one—right in the middle of a fairy tale," she answered, determined to hold the day's unpleasant memories at bay.

In the elevator, David leaned toward her with an appreciative whiff. "You smell wonderful," he said.

Seeing the women around them pretending so hard not to be listening, Katie suppressed a giggle. "Thank you," she said. "It's Joy!" she added, wondering how her fellow passengers would interpret that remark!

At the Antilles Lounge door they joined a long line of people waiting to be introduced to the captain and to have their pictures taken with him.

"Well, look who's together again!" Edwin Goodman said.

Ella nudged her husband. Curing him of his lack of tact appeared to be an impossible mission, Katie thought, although Ella accepted the challenge with good humor.

"You look wonderful!" Katie exclaimed. "Both of you!"

Edwin, in his black tuxedo, and Ella, slim and lovely in a sapphire blue gown, chatted happily about the island excursions. David, too, seemed to be enjoying the elderly couple.

The reception line moved slowly, but finally she and David were introduced to the captain, whose white uniform and Italian accent lent a special dash to the festivities. Flashbulbs flared, then they were in the lounge where formally-dressed waiters hovered with trays of drinks. On stage, the ship's orchestra played soft, romantic melodies.

As she and David sat down on a small gold velvet couch, she observed Giselle's spectacular entrance in a slinky black silk dress cut in a deep V nearly to her waist. She seemed oblivious to the stares as she floated into the lounge.

Stopping in front of David, Giselle purred, "I do hope you were saving this seat for *me*."

Katie watched helplessly as Giselle sat with fluid grace and whispered in his ear. David seemed perfectly at ease, responding with muffled laughter to a private joke. As they sat together, pressed close on the narrow couch, Katie speculated on their relationship. Giselle was glamorous, worldly-wise, an astute businesswoman. She and David shared a host of memories. It seemed natural that he should be drawn to someone so like his first wife. But Katie found herself pleading silently: *Please don't let him be in love with her!* and wondering why she allowed herself to care.

The scenario ended abruptly as one of the ship's officers crossed the room to ask Giselle to dance. He spoke in fluent French and she responded in kind. *"Mais oui!"* She rose to accompany the handsome officer to the dance floor.

Katie studied David's dispassionate look. It was impossible to tell if he minded Giselle's being swept away to the dance floor. For a moment Katie wondered if David would ask her to dance, but he only smiled down at her. Perhaps he didn't dance, she thought, remembering his slight limp. It didn't matter. It was a pleasure just to sit quietly alone with him.

Suddenly Katie wanted desperately for David to refute Giselle's warning. "Have you known Giselle long?" she asked.

He nodded, eyeing her curiously. "Nine years. Why do you ask?"

"You . . . seem like old friends."

"I suppose it depends on one's definition of the word *friend*," he answered.

Then maybe they *were* . . . romantically involved, she thought, and fought to hide her growing disappointment. "Gran Lucy, my grandmother, always says old friends, like old shoes, are best."

"Even old shoes can fall apart," David answered. "I guess I prefer Emerson's 'The only way to have a friend is to be one.'" He chuckled. "Now how did we ever get so terribly serious?"

Katie didn't respond, knowing very well that her curiosity about his relationship with Giselle had not been satisfied.

The ship's chimes rang out announcing dinner.

"You were right," she said. "Hearing those chimes does whet my appetite."

Laughing, they stood and merged with the crowd leaving for the dining room and the gala dinner.

"How elegant everyone looks tonight," she said.

"Clothes do make a difference," David agreed, "not only in appearance, but in bearing, in attitude."

"The ship is our stage and we're all playing parts?"

"Or life is a dream in the night?" he countered, with a smile.

She shrugged lightly. "I haven't thought about the meaning of life for such a long time," she heard herself saying.

"But you did once?" he asked, growing serious again.

"Yes. It seems a long time ago." When she was a freshman in high school, she had felt very close to God. It was when her mother's cancer had first been diagnosed. Instead of weeping in self-pity, her mother had calmly accepted the verdict. Later, she had even rejoiced at being ever closer to heaven.

At first Katie had been resentful, even skeptical of her mother's attitude. Then she found that the more she prayed, the more peaceful she felt, even as she dealt with the arrangements for her mother's imminent death. Praying for strength to go on, Katie had received it, along with a peculiar joy that illuminated the darkness surrounding her. Her church fellowship had offered support and practical assistance. It had been a time of great spiritual growth.

Then she had met Stan . . . After the long months of exhausting sickroom regimen and confinement, Katie welcomed his light-hearted approach to life. After dating him for several weeks, she began to sleep late on Sunday mornings, missing the church services. Gradually she had neglected reading the Bible at bedtime. Now she often failed to pray. Nor could she blame Stan for this spiritual lapse. She alone was responsible for her relationship with God.

As they stood at the dining room entrance waiting to be escorted in, Katie reflected on what David might think of Gran Lucy's philosophy—that the purpose of life was to glorify God.

"Impressive, isn't it?" David asked, gesturing toward the festive decorations. "A little touch of France."

Jolted into the present, she peered into the room. The draperies were closed, and the dining room glowed with candlelight. A profusion of French flags hung from the ceiling, giving the room a Continental look. Rumor had it that the dinner menu would offer excellent French selections.

As she and David stepped forward, the maitre d' smiled at them. *"Bon soir, mademoiselle et monsieur."*

"Bon soir," David responded.

Katie felt like true royalty as they were ushered to their dining room captain, who, in turn, escorted them to their candlelit table.

As she sat down, she noticed that the young Bowdens, totally engrossed in each other, had ordered an expensive bottle of wine. And the Zelts were already glassy-eyed from too many rum drinks. Walt, catching Katie's eye, winked at her.

"Bon soir, mademoiselle," the waiter said, presenting her with an oversized menu. The selections were staggering, and many of the dishes were listed in French. When David turned from discussing the menu with Giselle, Katie said with a hopeless laugh, "I don't know what to choose!"

"Do you like escargot?"

"I've never tried it." She knew only that escargot were snails, and that Stan had said that was where he drew the line with French cuisine. "I think I'll have the escargot," she found herself saying almost defiantly.

75

"You're sure?" David asked over his menu. The glow of candlelight accentuated his high cheekbones and angular chin. He was so striking that it took her breath away.

"Positive," she all but whispered.

He reached for her hand as if for a moment he, too, had forgotten that they were discussing dinner selections. "Would you like for me to order for you?" he asked.

"Yes, please." She noticed that Giselle was now watching them over David's shoulder, and the romantic interlude dissipated like flower petals scattering in a sudden chill wind. She reluctantly removed her hand from the warmth of his.

It was a moment before he averted his eyes, and she wondered how she appeared to him in the flattering light. Once, in the glow of candlelight, she had glimpsed herself in a darkly marbled mirror; it had been like seeing an ethereal shadow, a crinkled photograph taken in another lifetime, another era. She smiled at the memory.

"What's so amusing?" Mark Bowden asked her.

"Unreality," she answered. She remembered the children in the corridor calling her a princess and David a prince. "You know, the other side of the looking glass . . . fairy tales . . ."

Mark rubbed his bushy mustache, peering at her strangely. "I don't know much about that. I'm in the stock market. A broker."

Marcie Bowden leaned over her new husband, her auburn hair falling forward, her brown eyes intense. "He's very good at it too. You wouldn't believe how much money he made last year, even with the economy down."

Mark beamed.

Katie wondered whether their relationship centered around money. She hoped the sparks in their eyes were true love and not dollar signs.

Glancing at David, she reflected on her attraction to him. Was it his money? She didn't think so, although his lifestyle undoubtedly had its effect. Physical attraction? Partly—but she had been physically attracted to Stan too. Authority? Observing the finesse with which he dealt with people had aroused her admiration. There seemed to be more, she thought, as their eyes met again—something indefinable and just beyond her grasp.

"Penny for your thoughts," he challenged.

Daring to be honest, she said, "I was thinking about you."

"Positive or negative?"

"I don't know yet," she confessed, hoping that she hadn't backed herself into a difficult corner.

"How do I find out?"

Time, she thought, absorbed in the flickering candlelight. Even though she and David had known each other casually for several years, she suspected that it took a long time to know if one were really in love. Yet, ironically, some couples who lived together for a lifetime seemed not to possess that deep understanding and commitment that characterized the Goodmans' marriage, for instance. Perhaps it was a matter of time—and discernment.

David waved his fingers in front of her eyes. "Where did you go?"

She was grateful that there was no time for an answer. The waiter was serving her plate of escargot. The hot garlic butter smelled so tantalizing that her mouth watered. "It smells fantastic," she said, changing the subject.

David looked at her strangely, then turned to his escargot.

Katie watched as he and Giselle deftly manipulated the special metal utensil and tiny fork for extracting the meat from the escargot shell. She felt a bit clumsy at first, then became more adept. The first luscious bite made it well worth the trouble. "I had visions of my entire meal flying across the table," she confided to David and, following his lead, mopped up the buttery sauce with pieces of French bread.

"You're going to be a very expensive date for a fellow when we get home," he said. "We're spoiling you."

Darting a glance at him, she wondered if he meant fellows in general or himself, but his smile was so disarming that she thought he surely meant himself.

Giselle was holding forth with Bob and the Zelts about the Cordon Bleu classes she had taken in Paris. As they discussed their favorite Continental dishes, David joined in with enthusiasm. Again Katie felt terribly inadequate; her knowledge of gourmet cooking was limited, to say the least. Noting again her cabinmate's revealing neckline, she wished that Giselle were more modest in dress and less knowledgeable about French cuisine . . . and David!

From across the table, she saw Walt Zelt eyeing her, a knowing smile on his thin lips, and she quickly averted her gaze.

The waiter brought brown pottery bowls of French onion soup still bubbling under their thick golden crusts of cheese. Then a simple but delicious salad with vinaigrette dressing which, Giselle insisted, should have been served after their entrées in the French manner. "Why does everyone have to Americanize perfectly good French styles of eating?" she demanded in a huff.

For the main course David had chosen Boeuf Bourguignon, an aromatic beef stew cooked with red wine, onions, and mushrooms, and served over freshly made noodles. "It's the best thing I've ever eaten," Katie said as the tender meat shredded easily beneath her fork.

David looked pleased. "And you haven't had dessert yet. Mousseline au Chocolat. Chocolate mousse," he explained.

"I do know chocolate mousse," she replied. He must think her utterly uninformed.

Finally they stood up from the table. "I don't think I'll ever eat again," Mark Bowden vowed. He and Marcie, the Zelts, and Giselle were feeling the effects of the bottles of red wine they had consumed. Giselle, staggering slightly, reached for David's arm.

"I need a walk on deck," Katie interjected.

He turned to her immediately, leaving Giselle staring first in disbelief, then in fury.

She had purposely outmaneuvered Giselle, she thought, although she took no joy from it. Gran Lucy would say, "Do unto others as you would have them do unto you." The world seemed to say, "Do unto others before they can do you in!"

"We're going to get some fresh air," David called to Bob, who was heading for the Antilles Lounge for the after-dinner show. "Hold seats for us."

As David caught her hand in his, Katie felt a warmth surging through her. They moved through the crowd and beyond the elevators, walking up the stairwell to the Promenade Deck.

When they stepped outside, the moonlight seemed a surprise, a wonder. "I feel like Cinderella at the ball," she said.

"Maybe you are! The travel brochures call this ship a floating palace," David said smiling, still holding her hand.

A rush of tenderness flooded her as they walked to the railing, bringing back the memory of last night's kiss. She wanted more than anything to be in David's arms again. Instead, he dropped her hand and leaned against the railing, looking out at the star-spangled night.

"David . . ." she began softly, wanting to apologize again for her childish behavior earlier in the day.

"Would you like to walk?" he asked, indifferent to her mood.

She was so astonished that she nodded. Then they were walking briskly around to the gusty windward side of the ship. Katie tried vainly to secure her wildly blowing hair, thinking that either he was taking her quite seriously about needing fresh air or was not interested in a romantic encounter.

The wind made talk impossible, and she had to run to keep up with him. As they rounded the deck to the protected leeward side, she stopped. "Please let me catch my breath!"

"Sorry," he said amiably.

She searched the dark sky for the Milky Way. Finding it, her eyes traveled on. "Is there a name for those stars?" she asked, pointing to a cluster of brilliance near the horizon.

"The Pleiades," he said. "Also known as the Seven Sisters. They're supposedly the seven daughters of Atlas, pursued by the great hunter, Orion."

Did the seven sisters regret the fact that Orion never caught them? Katie mused. How she regretted running from David this morning as she thought of what might have been! Trying to recall the little Greek mythology she had learned, she asked, "Wasn't it Artemis, goddess of the hunt, who killed Orion and placed him in the sky as a constellation?"

"Most people don't know that. Now it's my turn to be impressed." David's look was frankly admiring.

Katie pressed her advantage. "Where is Orion?" she asked.

He placed an arm around her so she could see where he pointed. "The three bright stars to the left are Orion's belt. See the upraised sword in his hand?"

"Yes . . ." The musky scent clinging to his smooth-shaven jaw was intoxicating. Yet he seemed unmoved by her nearness when all she wanted now was to be in his arms.

"There, beneath the belt, you can see the Great Nebula in Orion," he continued. Suddenly he swept her into his arms, holding her tightly, his chin resting atop her hair, then just as quickly released her. "Let's go in," he said curtly.

His sudden change of mood was perplexing, and the silence between them grew as they took the elevator to the Antilles Lounge. He looked terribly serious, as if he had firmed his resolve and reached some kind of clear decision.

She tried to concentrate on the passenger capacity sign, but her heart plummeted more rapidly than the elevator.

When they stepped into the lounge, the show was beginning. On stage, the ship's combo filled the air with the African rhythms of calypso. Across the room, Bob stood to wave them over, and they made their way through the lively crowd to the place where he and Giselle were holding seats for them.

"Hi, David!" a breezy, young voice called from the seat behind them.

Katie bit her lip as she recognized the cute brunette who had hung on David's every word at the pool this afternoon. She smiled at him, secrets dancing in her eyes, her low-cut dress shimmering in the dim light.

David brightened. "Hi there, Darlene!" And he stepped aside to say something further, leaving the girl in gales of laughter. Katie could not bear the sudden stab of jealousy.

Returning to Katie's side, he said, "I'm getting into the calypso mood!" His mood seemed suddenly light and carefree.

The tour director, taking the microphone, spoke over the music. "Welcome to Calypso Night! But before this African-Caribbean style of jazz gets the better of you, we'd like to play a little game. Some of you singles are still not getting around, and, after all, the object of a cruise is to make friends . . . to have fun . . . Now I want every unattached woman in this room to hop up and kiss a stranger."

Katie sat back in dismay.

Suddenly there was a plump redhead running around the couch to kiss David. Darlene was right behind her, waiting her turn. Katie turned a disapproving look on the girls, but it didn't faze them.

Without warning, Walt Zelt pulled Katie from the couch and kissed her hard on the mouth. She was so flabbergasted that it took a moment before she could twist loose, sinking back onto the couch with David. She wanted to wipe Walt's wet kiss from her lips.

Walt laughed. "I couldn't let the opportunity pass by," he said on the way back across the aisle.

Beside her, Sondra Zelt was kissing Bob and then David.

The tour director yelled, "Enough! Enough! I didn't dream that under those quiet exteriors lurked savage jungle beasts!"

Katie was appalled that so many women . . . and Walt Zelt . . . would run around the room to kiss strangers, who possibly didn't even want to be kissed.

Onstage, the ship's combo began to play an old calypso tune, and the tour director introduced their entertainer of the evening.

The handsome black singer from Trinidad ran forward down the far aisle, taking the portable microphone, and stunning the audience with his honeyed voice. His style, as he moved around the stage, was unbelievably sensual, almost steamy. His voice, reminiscent of Harry Belafonte's, moved in counterrhythm to the music. Soon he had the audience clapping, alive with excitement, as he interspersed old favorites like "Yellow Bird" with salacious folk songs that all but sizzled as he played with the words.

Clapping to the earthy rhythms, David darted a glance at

Katie, capturing her hands in midair as their eyes locked. He seemed to whisper her name, and she was lost in the primal beat and in the passion in his eyes.

The singer swayed down the aisle toward them, the spotlight moving with him. His provocative intonations suffused his words with sensual meanings, ". . . daylight come and I wanna go home."

As the singer stopped before them, the spotlight held them in its brilliant beam, while the singer's words hung around them like molasses, ". . . daylight come, and I wanna go home . . ." He grinned, improvising to the melody, ". . . man, you bettah kiss dat woman now . . ." He stood waiting as he sang on, the spotlight fixed on them . . . and there was nothing to do but for David to kiss her.

His lips came down on hers possessively and, caught up in the music and the moment, she responded with abandon, not caring what the crowd might think, not caring about anything except the warmth of David's embrace. They were floating, spiraling away through the spotlight and the sultry rhythms until she was aware of nothing but David.

The crowd around them applauded, laughing, led by the singer, who nodded his approval in tempo with the music. Amazed, then embarrassed, Katie moved away from David.

". . . daylight come and I wan . . . na go home," the singer sang out and moved on with the spotlight.

As she sat back in the darkness, she felt as taut as the guitar strings pulsating with the calypso beat. She turned to look at David.

"Sorry!" he said harshly.

Sorry?! She hadn't felt a moment's regret—until now!

CHAPTER 6

THE NEXT MORNING Katie blushed furiously as she recalled the incident of the evening before. Just as Stan had used her to charm his clients for his own personal gain, she felt that David was amusing himself with her naïvete. Katie was certain now that she was a novelty with whom he would soon grow bored. He and Giselle had probably enjoyed a good laugh together after Katie rushed to her cabin—utterly mortified.

A kiss was a sacred thing, Katie believed, to be reserved for private moments and to be exchanged between two people who cared deeply for each other. Now she had dropped her guard more than once with David, overpowered by his irresistible good looks. But "beauty is only skin deep," as Gran Lucy had often reminded her, and who knew what lay beneath the surface of the enigmatic David Wallace. He was becoming a mystery she could not afford to unravel.

Slipping out of bed, she picked up the morning paper which the steward had slid under the cabin door. Not wanting to wake Giselle by turning on a light, she read by the shaft of sunshine streaming in through the porthole.

Under the column that listed the day's activities, she found a notice of the religious service held daily in the cinema. If she hurried, she could make both breakfast and the service. Having bungled things so badly, she was looking forward to a time to collect her thoughts.

At seven-thirty she stepped into the dining room. Only a few people were seated at each table. "Where is everyone?" she asked Ella and Edwin Goodman as the waiter seated her.

"Sleeping late, I expect," Edwin said, buttering a bran muffin. "Say, what happened to you last night after that big kiss?"

Katie swallowed, pretending to concentrate on the menu. "Nothing much. I was tired and went to bed."

"You shouldn't let such a big handsome guy like David out of your sight for long," Edwin said. "The girls were asking him to dance! In our day, you never saw anything like that!"

"Never mind, Edwin," his wife interrupted, but too late.

The words on Katie's menu blurred out of focus. She was aware of the waiter standing behind her now, taking in Edwin's last words. "Just the cantaloupe, please," she ordered, her tone a little less than composed.

"You'd better have something else too, honey," Ella urged.

"This will be more than enough." She could visualize the girls lined up waiting to dance with David. "Shameless," Gran Lucy would call them. It occurred to Katie that she had behaved just as shamelessly.

Looking up, she saw Walt Zelt strolling to the table alone.

He grinned widely. "Well, if it isn't the prettiest girl on

the ship," he said, sitting next to her. "Maybe the most passionate too."

She felt the hot flush rising as rapidly as her anger.

"Surprised me," he added. "I took you for one of those nice, quiet girls."

Katie pried the fluted paper from around her blueberry muffin, holding back her retort. She deserved his low opinion. But there was something about Walt that revolted her, an oiliness in his manner. More than that, he reminded her of dirty-mouthed school boys whose delight it was to shock girls.

It was unusual for her to take such an instant dislike to someone. Perhaps she was being unfair, she thought. Buttering a blueberry muffin, she listened to Walt discuss last night's events with the Goodmans. Evidently the gala had become even wilder as the evening progressed. David's kiss would not be the most memorable event.

"You're mighty quiet," Walt said to her after a while.

"I'm not awake yet," she answered and bit into the warm muffin.

Something brushed against her leg and for a moment she decided that it was her imagination. Moving her leg away slightly, she glared at Walt. His hooded eyes and complacent smile made it obvious that his leg against hers had been no accident.

She gulped her hot coffee, and rose to leave, waving to the Goodmans. Walt seemed amused. What she needed was some fresh air.

"What's wrong?" Walt asked with a chuckle.

"Excuse me, please," she said, getting up from the table.

Minutes later she stepped out on deck into the dazzling sunshine. She inhaled deeply, her anger beginning to dissipate. How different things appeared when one was surrounded by the perfection of God's creation. It was man who took that which is precious and beautiful, and tarnished it with greed and lust. A man like Walt Zelt.

As she stood at the railing, she realized that something had changed. Of course! Instead of a dark inky-blue color, the sea was vibrant turquoise. During the night they had sailed into the Caribbean.

The few passengers who were out on deck were exclaiming over the surprising turquoise sea. Others lay on lounges, reading or dozing. Two joggers made their way around at intervals.

Katie wandered to the back railing and stood watching as the ship pressed onward through the water. Behind her, the wake flared, sparkling like diamonds into white cresting waves, then smoothing again to a glassy stillness. Would her life be like the passage of this ship—temporarily disturbing the surface of things only to fade quickly, leaving no lasting imprint? She knew she wanted more—to probe the depths, to discover the treasure buried within her.

She had seen no other ships, and there had been no sign of birds or fish since they had left Florida. It seemed as if they were moving through the beginning of time, as if the earth had just begun. There was only the sky with its high, white puffy clouds, the turquoise sea, and the big white ship passing through.

Time seemed irrelevant as she stood there. Nothing seemed important except being a part of this moment in existence. When she did glance at her watch, she realized the service was already in progress.

By the time she reached the Continental Deck, she could hear the sounds of singing. The familiar hymn had once been a favorite of hers—"Sweet Hour of Prayer." Strange that she never found sweetness now in her occasional perfunctory prayers.

A smiling young woman handed her a hymnal already opened. "Second verse," she whispered.

Katie's voice, a mellow alto, joined with the others: "Sweet hour of prayer, sweet hour of prayer, Thy wings shall my petition bear, To Him whose truth and faithfulness engage the waiting soul to rest . . ."

Without warning, tears flooded her eyes. Though her voice quavered, the words were comforting: "And since He bids me seek His face, believe His word and trust His grace, I'll cast on Him my every care, and wait for Thee, sweet hour of prayer."

What was it about the words that had touched her so? She examined them again. "Thy wings shall my petition bear . . ."

"God inhabits the praise of His people," Gran Lucy always said. "Prayers move on wings of love, on that golden shaft of joy that opens when you praise Him. I don't believe prayers of desperation are nearly as effective."

Prayers of desperation . . . That described her prayer life lately, Katie thought miserably as she sat down.

The pastor stood before them. "Heavenly Father," he prayed, "most glorious Lord God, at whose command the winds blow and lift up the waves of the sea . . ."

Katie sensed the presence of someone standing beside her. For a moment, she hoped it was David, though she had no idea whether he was a believer.

The words of the hymn continued to haunt her. "I'll cast on Him my every care . . ." She had not cast her cares on God for some time. She tried to do everything herself as if she doubted His ability to handle her affairs.

The pastor's prayer was a paean in praise of the beauties of the earth, sky, and sea. When it was over, she opened her eyes to find Ella Goodman at her side as they sat down.

"God is love," the pastor said. "Love is patient and kind, never jealous or envious, never boastful or proud, never haughty or selfish or rude. Love does not insist on its own way. Love does not delight in evil, but will barely notice when others accidentally do wrong . . ."

Why couldn't she have recognized Stan's boastfulness and arrogance? He had been all pride, all ego, yet she had loved him so much. She had grown more and more like him, and now she was holding grudges against him.

The pastor continued. "If you love someone, you will be loyal no matter what the cost . . ."

Stan had been totally disloyal! Katie thought in dismay. He had only pretended to love; he had made a mockery of it, a sham, but perhaps it had been her fault too. Only love misused could destroy.

"We can see and understand only a little about God now," the pastor said. "It's as if we were peering at His reflection in a dim mirror. But someday we will see Him face to face. Then we'll see everything clearly, just as clearly as God sees into our hearts right now."

Katie wasn't sure that she wanted Him to see into her heart. She was still so full of bitterness about Stan—and now David.

"There are three things that remain," the pastor said, "faith, hope, and love—and the greatest of these is love. Let love be your greatest aim."

After the service, Ella said softly, "I knew you were a believer. I just had a feeling about you."

"I've been away from God, for a long time it seems, Ella. I've made such a mess of things."

"You're not alone," Ella said, collecting her handbag. "For a time I tried to run the world around me, and it almost ruined our marriage . . ."

"*Your* marriage?" Katie asked, astonished. "It seems so

solid. You two are so right for each other, so happy together."

"It wasn't always that way. I suppose that if divorces had been more popular when we were young, our marriage would have been another of the casualties," Ella said. "Instead of turning to a divorce court, which doesn't seem to settle much anyway, I got on my knees every day and turned everything over to God."

"What happened?" Katie asked.

"I slowly found peace . . . a deep serenity I'd never had before. And joy! I hadn't even known what the word meant." Ella paused, "And I learned about love."

"About love?" Katie echoed, not comprehending.

Ella nodded. "First I learned that I didn't have to *like* everyone or what they did. Then I found that I could love people who hadn't even seemed lovable before."

"What happened next?" Katie asked as they headed out of the theater, lagging behind the others.

"Next Edwin and I *really* fell in love." She laughed. "We'd been married for twenty years by then. Everyone thought that we'd gone crazy, holding hands and acting like newlyweds."

"Sounds wonderful!" Katie said.

"It was and it still is," Ella said. "I think that Edwin's actually relieved that I love Jesus more than I love him. Poor Edwin was tired of being my knight in shining armor, trying to be perfect. You see, I had made a god of him. I forgot that we were mere mortals. But we finally have our priorities straight."

They walked on in silence for a while.

"You love David, don't you?" Ella asked.

"I don't know. I don't want to, yet . . ." She stopped. "You see, I just broke an engagement a few months ago." She found herself confiding in Ella what she had told no one except Gran Lucy about Stan's unfaithfulness, her own hurt and bitterness.

The older woman raised her eyebrows. "Good thing that you found out before it was too late."

Katie dropped her head, anguish flooding her again. "I trusted him so much!" she blurted, struggling to control her emotions.

They stopped in front of the elevator and Ella pushed the button. "I trusted Edwin too," she said softly.

Katie was aghast. "Edwin?"

Ella smiled. "We were young once, you know, and temptation is always lurking around the next corner. Another girl. Another man. I expect that it's always been like that."

Katie nodded. "It's just that I can't trust men at all anymore." She thought about Stan and David . . . and Walt Zelt only this morning.

"I suppose it's going to take some time, Katie," Ella said. "What you're going to have to do first, though, is to trust God."

The elevator doors opened, ending their conversation. As Katie stood in the elevator she wondered, *How can I learn to trust God again when I haven't trusted Him for so long?*

CHAPTER 7

IN THE CABIN Giselle still slept soundly.

Katie changed into her swimsuit and cover-up. She slipped her paperback book into her handbag and stepped into the corridor.

"Katie?"

She stopped at the sound of David's low voice, not turning, trying to compose herself as he caught up with her. He was dressed for sunbathing in a white terry cloth beach jacket and blue trunks.

"Going to catch some sun?" he asked, looking as if the incident of the evening before had been erased from his memory.

"Yes," she replied, with cool restraint.

"Interested in some company?" he asked.

"Why not?"

Any woman sitting beside him last night could just as easily have been the recipient of that passionate kiss, inspired by the sensual music and the insistent singer. As for that first night . . . an honor bestowed on the newest member of the agency? A memory to pack away with other mementos of the trip? A natural outcome of moonlight and mood music? After all, he *was* a man, and men seemed to share a number of disturbing similarities.

Passing the children's drawings in the corridor, she glanced into the youth activity room. The two children sat with a group busily creating other artistic masterpieces.

"Look!" the little boy said. "It's the prince and princess!"

"Hi, kids!" David called as they waved their greeting.

Katie had enjoyed the pleasant interlude with the children, but they belonged to another woman. The entire evening had been a fairy tale . . . just a glamorous gala aboard a cruise ship. It had nothing to do with reality.

Down below on the Promenade Deck, late risers were served a continental breakfast from the buffet tables.

"Have you eaten?" David asked.

"Yes. In the dining room."

"Good girl," he said. "I'm afraid I just got up."

Not very surprising, she thought, as she settled on one of the lounges near the pool. Obviously, after she had left, he had partied late into the night. And if he cared for her at all, he wouldn't have risked hurting her by bringing that fact to her attention.

She took off her beach cover-up and sat down on the lounge, aware that David was admiring her trim figure. The look on his face was undisguised male appreciation. She may not have the generous curves of a Giselle, nor would she display them so flamboyantly, but she was beautifully proportioned and her modest swimsuit revealed the lovely lines of her body.

David appropriated the adjacent lounge, removing his beach jacket, while Katie slathered herself with suntan lotion, far too aware of how attractive he was.

"Can I get you anything from the buffet?" he asked, standing over her.

Disconcerted by his nearness, she answered, "Yes . . ."

He smiled. "Yes, what?"

"Just orange juice," she said, quickly pulling out her book and opening it.

When he returned, she was engrossed in the story.

By eleven o'clock all the chaises on deck were occupied, and the smell of suntan lotion mingled with the salty tang of the air. Katie brushed away the moisture from her upper lip. "Think I'll take a dip."

"It's a salt-water pool," he cautioned. "You'll ruin your hair."

"It's washable," she laughed, guessing that Eva and the glamorous girls he dated were overly concerned about their appearance.

"I'm glad you don't melt," he said, getting up with her.

She cast about for a retort. "I have to wash my hair for the Wallace-Tyler party this afternoon anyhow," she stated flatly.

She ran to the pool, the deck hot under her feet, but not so fast that she didn't notice Darlene and the other girls who had surrounded him on the deck yesterday. They watched him now, their eyes filled with admiration. She didn't even want to see how David dealt with their attention. Stan would have played it to the hilt to arouse her jealousy.

Noting again the "No Diving" sign, she decided it was posted because of the constant sloshing of water. All three of the ship's swimming pools were surrounded by tile decks and two-foot decorative walls. Despite the enclosures, water often splashed over them, sending squealing sunbathers fleeing.

"I thought the Caribbean was supposed to be smooth," she said.

"There's probably a storm brewing somewhere," David responded.

Grabbing the handrails, she stepped into the pool. "The water is so warm!"

"It not the Pacific," he laughed, waiting for her to move away from the ladder.

She pushed off with a breaststroke in the buoyant salt water, then suddenly realized how little control she had. As the water tossed from one end of the pool to the other, she was lifted like a goldfish in a slowly tilted bowl.

"This is fun!" she called back to David.

"It's different," he admitted as he swam toward her. "But I like a little more control over my direction."

She considered his words in light of this morning's religious service. How much control did most people have over their direction in life?

As they lolled about in the pool, the swells increased, but the swimmers took the unpredictable shifts with good humor. Several clambered out after a particularly violent splash, while others climbed in to take their places.

Suddenly a huge swell lifted the ship, bouncing the swimmers across the pool, then heaved them forcefully at the wall. For an instant Katie was certain she would crash against the tiling, but David grabbed her, hauling her to safety.

"We'd better get out," he warned. "It's getting dangerous."

As he pulled her behind him toward the ladder, the water surged back, carrying them with it. With the force of a powerful undertow, they were thrust toward the pool wall once again. At the last moment David braced himself in front of her, taking the full blow on his back as the water pressed her heavily against him. She could only stare helplessly, her eyes wide. As the water shifted once again, he helped her up the ladder and followed quickly.

The ship's general alarm bells rang, and an announcement crackled over the loudspeaker. "Since we are experiencing heavy swells, we ask that all swimmers vacate the pools. We repeat: Swimmers vacate the pools."

They stood for a moment, catching their breath and licking the salt from their lips.

"High adventure! Just what the brochures promised!" David teased to ease the tension, brushing his wet hair from his face.

"Almost too much," Katie replied, remembering with embarrassment the instant she had been pressed into David's arms by the restless water. But he seemed strangely composed and unaffected by their intimate encounter.

Seating herself on the chaise lounge, Katie coiled her wet hair and fastened it on top of her head. Newly aware of David's presence, she couldn't return to her reading and was frustrated to see that he had rolled over onto his stomach and had apparently fallen asleep. She applied a liberal coat of suntan lotion, wishing that she could escape her turbulent emotions so easily.

It seemed only moments later that she heard David's voice calling her name. "Katie!"

He was moving slowly toward her through a crowded room, much like an airport terminal, searching the faces in the crowd. She was trying to reach him, to let him know that she was coming—but her legs were immobilized in warm liquid . . .

"Katie! Wake up! You're going to burn."

She opened her eyes, feeling the heat on her back and legs, tasting the brine on her dry lips. Raising her head, she found David watching her with concern.

"I hated to awaken you, but your back is turning red," he explained.

She blinked groggily and rolled over. "What time is it?"

"Twelve-thirty. Time to eat again."

"Oh, no!" She sat up, smiling sleepily.

"The good news is that the buffet lines are down to a reasonable wait," he said.

"I feel too lazy to move," she said, reaching for her cover-up. She noticed that he had donned his beach jacket. Good! She felt far more comfortable.

"Let's eat," he said heartily and pulled her to her feet.

In the buffet line, they found Bob Tyler. "Where's Giselle?" he asked. "I haven't seen her all day."

"She was still in the cabin sleeping when I changed around nine-thirty," Katie said. "Something wrong?"

"No," Bob said. "It's just that I hear she tottered in last night about four o'clock, and I was hoping that she'd help with this afternoon's party. Seems she had a little too much to drink. She's been known to be incapacitated the day after."

Katie ignored the remark and turned her attention to the sumptuous buffet set up in the shade of the overhang. The aroma of fried chicken, Italian sausages, meat balls, fish, lasagna, spaghetti, and meat loaf wafted from the enormous stainless steel serving dishes. There were salad bar makings as well as fruit salads, cole slaw, macaroni and carrot salads, and a luscious assortment of desserts.

"Come join us, Bob," David invited as their plates were filled by attendants.

"No, thanks. I'm on the Sun Deck with a good book."

"And a bevy of beautiful women, I'll bet!" teased David.

"Yep!" Bob grinned. "But none of them are my type."

It was strange to hear them bantering about women, Katie thought as she placed a glass of iced tea on her tray. Did they ever discuss her? Compare her with Giselle?

They were laughing again and she looked at Bob intently. With his sandy hair and boyish good looks, he was certain to attract many women, but she had the impression that he wasn't in the mood now. She recalled that at work he'd occasionally shown interest in her . . .

"See you later," Bob said and disappeared up the steps to the deck above.

"I wonder if anyone is eating lunch in the dining room today?" Katie asked. "It would be a shame to pass up this sunshine."

David nodded. "It couldn't be more perfect."

"No," she agreed. *It couldn't be more perfect.* She looked at him, wondering what he had meant, but his dark glasses masked his expression. Luncheon tray in hand, they wound their way back through the scattered lounges. As they ate, they chatted about the afternoon's party for clients and the island tours ahead. She was happy and fulfilled and knew that the dazzling warmth she felt had nothing to do with the sunshine.

"Time for me to wash my hair for the party," she said later, reluctant to leave.

"Why don't you try the beauty salon?"

She hesitated, not wanting to admit that her budget didn't allow for such luxuries.

"Just charge it to your cabin," he said, as if guessing her dilemma. "We'll consider it a company expense since you are playing hostess."

On the Ocean Deck, she found the salon easily. An hour and a half later, Katie marveled at the transformation wrought by the deft fingers of the British hairstylist. Her hair had been swept back, dipping slightly over the left eye, then pulled to one side to tumble in a heavy curl to her shoulder. A few errant tendrils had escaped to float provocatively around her face. Feminine. Definitely feminine.

"It's a distinctive look with that thick, dark hair of yours, ducks," the woman said. "Lovely, if I do say so myself."

Later, in her room, Katie had less than a half-hour to dress. She slipped into a white-on-white striped linen, its square-cut bodice appliqued with tiny flowers. She daubed a drop of Joy behind each ear and at the pulse point of her wrists.

Suddenly the cabin door opened. "Well, if you aren't the picture of the ingénue," Giselle smirked.

Katie managed a smile. Maybe she didn't look sophisticated, but, if clothes made a statement, the simple white dress said that this was a lady, not a swinger. She picked up her small clutch purse. "Aren't you going to the Wallace-Tyler party?" she asked Giselle, who was changing back into her nightie.

"I'm not feeling well," Giselle said. Her face was pale.

"What's wrong?"

"Motion sickness. The doctor gave me a shot and some pills. I can't help with the party."

"Is there anything I can do for you?" Katie asked with concern.

"Yes," Giselle yawned and turned away. "Let me sleep."

Katie closed the door softly.

Arriving in the Calypso Lounge a few minutes early, she found David and Bob there ahead of her. "Giselle can't make it," Katie said. "She's ill." The two men exchanged glances.

"Well, *you* look cool and crisp," observed Bob.

Katie laughed. "Giselle's word for it is *ingénuous!*"

"Aren't you?" David asked, leaving her to guess which definition he had in mind—*naïve, simple, trusting, innocent . . . ?*

David and Bob were genial hosts, and Katie loved playing hostess to the Californians who had flown out with them. Nearly everyone attended the party, many of them delightful older clients like the Goodmans who were enjoying every moment of the trip. Waiters hovered solicitously with refreshing beverages and elegant canapés made in the ship's kitchens.

The party was nearly over when Katie noticed Walt Zelt heading in her direction. She quickly glanced around to find David watching closely from across the room. She smiled and tried to walk leisurely to his side.

"Having fun?" he asked, his eyes focusing just over her shoulder.

"Wonderful!" she exclaimed. When she turned, she saw that Walt had followed her.

"Well, if it isn't the passionate couple," he jibed.

David ignored the rude comment. "Are you having a good time, Walt?"

"Not as good as you two, I'll bet," Walt replied.

A muscle in David's jaw tightened. "I think you have the wrong idea," he said, grabbing Walt by the elbow. "Here, let me get you a fresh drink."

Katie was astonished to see how adroitly David maneuvered the heavy, older man through the crowded room to his wife, who appeared a bit dazed from too many drinks. Despite her irritation, Katie nearly laughed.

"Good party, wasn't it?" Bob asked, as the congenial crowd thinned.

"I thought so," David agreed. "What about you, Katie?"

"A smash!" she said. "Everyone had such a fine time that I'm sure they'll be booking another cruise with Wallace-Tyler."

"Spoken like a true travel agent!" The men smiled their approval. Then, arm-in-arm, they headed for the Mediterranean Lounge to recap the events of the afternoon and to enjoy the stylistic piano renditions. Before long the dinner chimes sounded.

As they were escorted into the dining room, Katie thought what a pleasure it was to be sharing the evening with David and Bob. There was something touching about their friendship—the playfulness of small boys, with overtones of greater depths of mutual understanding. They had clearly experienced both good and difficult times together. If anything, Bob seemed somewhat protective of David— perhaps a result of the accident in which he had been the driver, Katie mused.

In the dining room, the Zelts were already seated. Walt rose slightly and somewhat unsteadily from his chair, his eyes glittering as he looked at Katie. She was glad to be sitting safely between David and Bob. Something about Walt Zelt frightened her.

"There's an Agatha Christie movie on tonight," Bob said.

"How about it, Katie?" David asked. "Will you join us?"

"Delighted," she said. She sat back to enjoy the informal dinner which was delicious without being a major production. She noticed, too, that with Giselle absent, all three of them seemed more relaxed.

After the movie, they stopped in the Antilles Lounge to watch the floor show, a country singer and a comedian. The only sour note of the evening was when David and Bob escorted Katie back to her cabin. She was surprised to see Walt Zelt in the corridor. For some reason, she hadn't known that the Zelt's cabin was on the Europa Deck.

"Good night, Katie," David and Bob said as she let herself into the cabin.

"Thanks for a lovely evening," she said.

Giselle was in bed sleeping peacefully. Latching the chain securely, Katie wondered about Walt Zelt's reaction to the threesome. Whatever it was, she was sure to hear from him later.

CHAPTER 8

KATIE AND BOB TYLER stood at the railing of the Promenade Deck, looking out at the magnificent stormy seascape. Billowing gray clouds blotted out large portions of the blue sky.

"Surely it wouldn't rain for our first stop, would it?" Katie fretted as the ship plowed across the open sea toward the island they would visit in the Netherlands Antilles.

Bob appeared unconcerned. "October storms usually blow through quickly here."

A fat drop splatted on Katie's forehead, then another on her bare arm. Suddenly rain splattered loudly on the deck, starting a run for cover by everyone.

"It'll be over in a few minutes," Bob said as they stood watching from under an overhang.

Noticing wet splotches on her white blouse and old brown culottes, she was glad that she had decided on a practical outfit for the day. Her culottes would be comfortable for climbing in and out of the small boat that would tender them from the Golden Renaissance to the dock at St. Maarten.

Her white sandals would be sensible for walking, and her hair was held back by a huge tortoise shell barrette that Gran Lucy had given her. For fun, gold hoop earrings dangled at her ears.

She wiped the dark drops from the brown plastic cover of the small camera hanging from her neck. The fragrance of Joy on her wrists and behind her ears seemed intensified by the warm rain. She wondered if Bob knew that David had given the perfume to her.

"We'd better eat inside," Bob said when it appeared that the rain was not going to stop. They joined the throng of passengers who had made the same decision and rushed for the elevators and stairs.

In the dining room, Katie looked for David, but he had received a radiogram from the Los Angeles office. Evidently it required an immediate reply. As she sat down at the table, the Zelts approached.

"Let's sit over here," Walt said to the waiter, indicating the two empty chairs beside Katie.

"Ready for our first port?" Walt asked as he sat down heavily.

"All set."

"I thought you'd be bursting with enthusiasm." He glanced around. "But then your lover boy isn't here."

She bristled at the insinuating term. "I beg your pardon." She hoped Bob would come to her rescue, but he was discussing something with Giselle.

"Isn't David your lover boy?" Walt asked so loudly that diners at the next table turned to listen. "Maybe you're not the sweet little thing you pretend to be," he continued with a grin. "Maybe Bob is your lover boy too."

It was all she could do to refrain from slapping him. "It isn't any of your affair!" she blurted, then regretted her unfortunate choice of words.

He laughed.

"Is that husband of mine giving you a bad time?" Sondra Zelt asked with a sigh. "You just ignore him, honey." She patted her hand. "Actually, he only bothers the pretty girls."

Ella Goodman caught Katie's eye across the table, sending her a consoling look. Then the waiter was handing out menus.

Later, hurrying outside to the Promenade Deck, she was delighted to find that the rain had stopped. Overhead, the clouds parted, giving way to patches of blue. Despite the wet deck, an expectant crowd stood at the railing, waiting for a glimpse of the green, hilly island on the port side.

The first sighting of land since leaving the Florida coast brought a spontaneous burst of applause. In the tropical sunlight, St. Maarten glowed like an emerald, set in turquoise sea and alabaster sky. It was a sight well worth the wait.

"That you, Katie?" A tremor of joy stirred as she heard David's pleasant, rumbling voice. "Where have you been all day?" he asked, carrying a handful of cookies to the railing.

"I slept late," she explained sheepishly. "And then gobbled lunch in the dining room."

"Have some dessert then." He offered some of the cookies, and she selected one with chocolate chips. At that moment David reminded her of a small boy—a boy who might have raided Gran Lucy's cookie jar.

They stood watching as sailors rode down in one of the covered lifeboats being lowered to the water alongside the ship. Near the bow, the gangway moved into position.

"Guess we'd better head down and get in line," David said, grabbing another handful of cookies from the buffet table. "Everyone seems to think that if you're not on the first boat tendering to the dock, the island is likely to disappear."

The loudspeaker announced, "Now cleared to land passengers."

Down on the Riviera Deck, Katie and David joined the milling crowd moving out to the gangway which led steeply downward to a small boat below. Katie clung tightly to the handrails, noticing in the distance that one of their tender boats was already halfway to the dock. At the bottom, a crewman helped her into the boat. David was close behind.

"Over here!" Bob called out from his seat near the front. No sooner had they taken their places near Bob and Giselle than the small vessel was underway—a mere speck beside the Golden Renaissance.

"Something happen between you and Walt at the table today?" Bob asked Katie.

David turned to hear her reply, but she shook her head nervously. Glancing about the boat, she was glad the Zelts had not boarded. When she looked out across the water toward St. Maarten, she found David studying her curiously.

Pulling her camera from the case, she began to snap pictures of the glorious seascape—above, the rain-washed sky ablaze with sunlight; below, a hundred small sailboats gliding like white butterflies on the turquoise sea; and, in the distance, the luxuriant green hills of the island beckoning in welcome.

"It's beautiful!" she whispered reverently to David when she was seated.

"*You're* beautiful!" he said, leaning forward to catch her hand in his. Her heart pounded wildly, but at a wry look from Giselle, he dropped her hand and turned to view the port town of Philipsburg.

Nearing the dock, a woman read from the tour excursion sheet: "This island has been peacefully divided between Holland and France for over three hundred years. Philipsburg is the capital of the Dutch portion of the island of St. Maarten; the Dutch spelling the name of the island with two a's; the French, with one. Otherwise the differences are few . . ."

On the dock, the tour director called out, "Half an hour till the buses leave from the main street! Yacht cruise people can assemble over by the tour sign!"

Katie's legs bounced strangely under her as she walked across the dock. "It's moving!" she said, steadying herself by clinging to David's arm.

"It's your sea legs," David laughed. "We haven't walked on land for three days."

On the other hand, Giselle, wearing a low-necked, black T-shirt and scanty white shorts, seemed unaffected by the days aboard ship. With her blond hair pulled back into a Grecian fall, she looked fresh and alluring.

"I loathe bus tours," Giselle said, as they headed for the painted archway spelling out "Warm Greetings."

"Should have taken the catamaran tour," Bob shrugged.

"I took it last year," Giselle answered. "Anyway I wanted to be with you handsome men."

David and Bob chuckled, but Katie saw nothing funny about it.

The four of them stepped under the welcoming archway into the city of Philipsburg. Just beyond was a small white clapboard courthouse, only two stories high. Except for louvered shutters at the windows and nearby palm trees, the building resembled many pictures she had seen of New England architecture. A brown shingled church with a steeple was distinguished by unique white shutters that flared outward like angels' wings.

The narrow main street, jammed with cars, was a succession of cafés and tourist shops with Dutch names like "Natraj." Katie lingered at the window of a linen shop, spying a lace tablecloth for Gran Lucy, then followed the others down the street.

"What do you think of it?" David asked Katie.

"It's not at all what I expected."

"Tourist trap," Giselle said shortly.

Wandering back to the corner where they were to catch the bus, they passed the linen shop again. "Do you think there's time to shop?" Katie asked. "That tablecloth looks perfect for my grandmother's big, round table."

Giselle glanced at it in the shop window. "You'll do better in St. Thomas."

Katie bit her lip. She should have known better than to ask. Perhaps Giselle was right, but she had a way of making Katie appear so foolish.

On the bus Giselle maneuvered a seat beside David, forcing Katie to take the next vacant seat where she was joined by an elderly lady. The door flapped shut, and the bus jerked forward.

As they drove past the small downtown area, the driver turned on the microphone: "Welcome to St. Maarten," he said. "Unfortunately, on this humid day, our air-conditioner is not working . . ."

This announcement was met with loud moans, and Katie heard Giselle's "I'll bet!" from two seats away.

Katie opened her window wider. As the bus gained speed and headed for the green hills, the breeze was pleasant. The sun warmed her arm, though her spirits were chilled by visions of Giselle's hand resting possessively on David's arm, of her golden legs bare beside him.

Curving through the open country and small villages, the driver pointed out the Great Salt Pond and other sites of interest as well as the magnificent vistas of green hillsides jutting into the turquoise Caribbean.

At International Point, most of the passengers climbed out to take pictures. Katie focused her camera on a velvety finger of land reaching out into the sea, then beyond to other distant islands.

She noticed that Giselle and David were not taking pictures, and, when they all climbed back on the bus, the woman sitting next to Katie said loudly, "I thought the tall, dark-haired fellow was your husband. Guess I was wrong."

Katie turned bright red. "No, we're all just friends."

Later, the bus descended to the French side of the island and they drove into the capital town of Marigot.

"This is more like it," Giselle said, loudly enough to be heard. "At least the atmosphere is a bit French."

Though the shops and houses bore a distinct aura of New Orleans, at least from what Katie had seen in pictures, she did not think them superior to the architecture on the opposite side of the island.

She followed the other passengers out for the half-hour rest stop, feeling increasingly forsaken as she was separated from the others by the crowd.

"We're going to have something cool to drink," Bob called to her as the three of them started out toward an outdoor café just above the town. It was a dubious invitation at best, and Katie had the distinct feeling that she was somehow intruding. Giselle talked rapidly, pointing out the sights. How enthralled David seemed with her!

Halfway up the small hill, David turned back, still laughing at a remark Giselle had made. "Aren't you coming, Katie?"

She nodded and followed them to the white clapboard café with its green-painted trim and trailing greenery. This was the man who had held her hand just a short time ago and called her beautiful. Was Giselle hearing the same words?

Bob stood under a white wooden canopy at the service counter. "What would you like?" he asked.

"Soft drink, please," she said, waiting with him while the busy counterman opened the bottles.

She had already seen David and Giselle in rapt conversation at one of the umbrella tables, and she hesitated, fearing that she might interrupt something. But Bob was carrying the tray of drinks to the table and there was nothing for Katie to do but follow. However, she was determined not to sit next to David and took the white metal chair near Giselle.

As she sipped her fruit drink, she realized that she had made a serious blunder. Next to Giselle, who looked cool and immaculate, she must appear wind-blown and travel-stained in her old clothes. She tried to smooth back the damp hair that had curled loose from her barrette. Worse still, she felt a headache lurking behind her eyes and fumbled in the bottom of her handbag for her aspirin tin.

"You all right, Katie?" Bob asked, sitting back after a sip of Coke.

"Just a little headache," she said, swallowing the aspirins that threatened to catch in her throat.

The shade, created by lush foliage trailing from the rooftops and trellises, offered some relief from the heat, and Katie was grateful for the brief respite. David and Giselle continued their discussion of ideas for Caribbean travel for Wallace-Tyler clients, punctuated by an occasional burst of laughter as they recalled other trips.

"Nice view," Bob said, motioning to the scene behind her.

Moving her chair so she could snap pictures allowed Katie to screen out the sight of the two so obviously enjoying their conversation. Indeed, the scene below was breathtaking. Palm trees descended the hill, with the vegetation growing all the way to the water's edge. In the bay, sailboats lay at anchor. It was a tranquil sight in sharp contrast to the turmoil building within her.

"Let's check out the shops," Giselle said after a while.

"I suppose we ought to," David agreed.

Katie's head throbbed so now that she begged off.

"I'd rather sit too," Bob said as Giselle and David rose from the table.

Katie realized there was nothing she could do to change the circumstances. Later, from her vantage point above the main street, she watched David following Giselle from one shop to another, interested and attentive.

When the four returned to the tour bus, it was a strained reunion, Katie felt. Though her headache had subsided, Giselle had succeeded in commanding David's full attention, occasionally touching his arm to emphasize a point.

The rest of the tour, though there was much of interest to see and record on film, was wasted on Katie. The ache in her heart was not lessened by the beauty of the scenery, and it was almost a relief to return to the main street where they had begun their tour a few hours earlier.

"We have until ten-thirty," David said, checking his watch. "Giselle and I thought we ought to check out the bistros for tourist action. How about it?"

Bob shook his head. "Sorry. This darn climate has gotten the best of me. I'm going back to the ship for a siesta."

Returning to the ship with Bob seemed a perfect out for Katie as well. At least she could lick her wounds alone and take a nap. "Think I'll go back too," she said and glanced away from David quickly as tears threatened to spill.

"Are you sure?" he asked.

"Yes." She blinked hard and smiled. With a fast wave, she headed down the street.

"I have to pick up something in a store," Bob called out behind her. "Can you get back all right?"

"Of course!" She saw Bob's worried expression, but noticed that Giselle and David were already setting off, her arm in his.

Katie hurried through Philipsburg's welcoming arch and toward the dock, her heart so full of anguish that she felt physically ill. She saw that one of the Golden Renaissance tenders was nearly full of passengers and hurried through the throng of people waiting on the dock.

"Going back?" one of the ship's crew asked, as she rushed toward them.

"Yes . . ."

"Just in time," he said with an Italian accent. "Room for only one more here." He helped her aboard, then the tender was shoved off from the dock.

Back in her cabin, Katie decided that she must be the only young single taking an afternoon nap, but she was exhausted—wrung out from the humidity and her emotional turmoil. As she climbed into bed, the last thing she recalled was Giselle holding David's arm as they set off down the street in Philipsburg. Then she drifted off into troubled sleep.

It seemed days later when she heard a knock at the cabin door. Blinking awake, she finally realized where she was. "Just a minute!"

She opened the door, peering around it in her yellow cotton nightie.

Bob stood in the corridor with a large package under his arm, an apologetic smile on his lips. "Are you all right? I was worried when you skipped dinner."

She nodded groggily, her long hair tumbling about in disarray. "What time is it?"

"Eight-thirty. Look, maybe I shouldn't have awakened you . . ."

"No, I'm glad you did. Otherwise I'd be waking up in the middle of the night."

Bob slipped the package through the partly-open door. "It's a present for you," he said.

"Oh, Bob . . . But why?"

"Consider it a bonus," he answered. "Listen, there's a beachcomber party tonight and a barbecue on deck. You won't believe what they've done . . . brought in palm fronds from St. Maarten and even sand. I thought you wouldn't want to miss it."

Katie glanced at the box. "Thank you. And thanks for the invitation. It'll take only a few minutes to dress."

His blue eyes sparkled. "I'll wait in my cabin," he said. "Just knock when you're ready."

Dropping the box on her bed, Katie hurried to the bathroom to take a quick shower. She did feel better, she thought gratefully.

Opening her closet, she pulled out a long yellow-and-white flowered shift, slit to the knees on both sides. It looked comfortable and smart with her white sandals. She brushed her hair so that it curled simply at her shoulders and was surprised at how refreshed she looked. Suddenly she remembered the box on her bed.

The name and Philipsburg address of a Dutch shop on the box were useless clues to its contents. Removing the lid, she was amazed to find the magnificent ecru lace-and-linen tablecloth from the shop window! Gran Lucy would love it!

She grabbed her key and handbag, and hurried to Bob's door. When he opened it, she felt like hugging him.

"Bob, what a thoughtful thing for you to do! It's beautiful, just perfect. But I want to pay you for it. How did you ever guess the right size?"

He closed his cabin door behind him and started down the corridor with her. "You said a big, round table, and the saleswoman said this was for a big, round table that seated eight or ten."

"It's exactly right. But why?"

Bob hesitated a moment before answering, "I've been learning lately that when you see something you really want, you should go after it. If you wait too long, it's apt to be gone."

Katie darted a sideways glance at him. She had the definite impression that he was not discussing tablecloths.

As they stepped out the aft door into the moonlight on the Europa Deck, Katie marveled at the sight. Down below on the Ocean and Promenade Decks, the railings were lined solidly with palm fronds; even the ship's deck-support posts had been wired with fronds and fashioned into palm trees. An elaborate fountain spouted from the middle of the empty swimming pool, and romantic music swirled from the ship's orchestra. Colored spotlights transformed the scene into an island fantasy.

"I'm not sure if it's supposed to be Caribbean or Hawaiian," Bob said as the tour director handed them each a plastic lei. "Either way, it should be easy to get into the spirit of things."

All the tables seemed to be occupied, and people were standing around the crowded dance floor; it looked impossible to find empty seats.

"Katie! Bob!" Ella Goodman called out from one of the tables under a newly-created palm tree.

They made their way through the festive crowd to join the older couple.

"Thanks," Katie said, noting the perplexed look on Ella's face. She knew that Ella was trying to decide what might be going on now. She knew only that Bob was her boss.

"Where's the rest of your gang?" Edwin asked.

Katie hoped that Bob would answer and looked at him.

"They're out casing St. Maarten for the tourist trade. We were too tired."

"I slept nearly four hours," Katie said quickly and thought Ella looked relieved.

"You must have needed it, dear," Ella said.

A waiter stopped by for their drink order, and the Goodmans excused themselves to stroll around the deck. Bob and Katie sat back to enjoy the balmy breezes and the music.

After a while Bob asked, "Dance?"

She shook her head. "No, thanks, but I'd love to walk." She hated herself for wishing it were David with whom she was sharing this romantic moonlight night.

They circled the deck slowly. Something about the moonlight and the island atmosphere made her feel deliciously languid, and she put aside all thoughts of David and Giselle. The thing to do was to enjoy this evening, she told herself. She would probably never experience such a special setting again in her lifetime.

"What are you thinking about so seriously?" Bob asked as they stopped by the railing to gaze up at the velvety sky.

Katie looked at him, thinking what an attractive man he was. "That I'm having a marvelous time." It occurred to her that under different circumstances, she might have been interested in a man like Bob.

"So am I," he said. They stood listening to the distant sentimental tunes played by the ship's orchestra. "What do you think of me, Katie?" he asked.

The unexpected question startled her, and she tried to hide her surprise. "That you're intelligent, attractive, kind . . ." She remembered the tablecloth. "And very considerate!"

He didn't answer, his thoughts far away.

Katie wondered again about the status of his marriage.

Word had it that his wife, Suzanne, was far more interested in advancing her career than their marriage.

"What do you mean by 'attractive'?" he asked.

She looked up at him, smiling indulgently. If he needed affirmation, that would be easy enough. "Tall, big shoulders, nice smile. To put it in one highly overused word—*handsome!*"

"You honestly think so?"

She nodded. *"I* think so. I suspect that *most* women would think so."

He was quiet for a moment. "I've never especially felt that way."

"But why not? It's true."

"I was one of those late bloomers," he said. "I grew up so darn fast all at once . . . all tall and gangly. My mother says I looked my best before five and after twenty-eight."

Katie sympathized with the insecure child within him—not so very different from her own fears of inadequacy. Strange how people viewed themselves.

"Katie . . ." he began, looking into her eyes. He caught her hands in his. "Do you think . . ."

"Yes?" She pulled away slightly, her breath in her throat, half dreading the question that seemed inevitable.

Diverted by a movement on the deck above, he dropped her hands. "Never mind," he said morosely, turning to brood into the darkness.

Katie lifted her eyes to the Europa Deck. Looking down from the railing were David and Giselle.

CHAPTER 9

STEPPING INTO THE dining room for breakfast, Katie glanced out the wide windows and caught glimpses of the green island of Antigua in the distance. The Golden Renaissance was to dock promptly at eight o'clock this morning. Apparently they would be on time again.

Bob, the Goodmans, and the Bowdens were already eating breakfast. She wondered where David was, then reminded herself that it really was not her concern; nothing about him was her concern. The idea of his deserting her for Giselle on St. Maarten still rankled, but her logic argued: *He's a free man, Katie. He hasn't uttered one word of commitment. He hasn't even said he loves you.*

"Good morning," Bob said, rising from his chair with the gentle smile she had come to expect from him. "I didn't think you'd make it down in time for breakfast."

"Barely," she admitted. "Giselle's having breakfast sent to the cabin, then she's taking the cruise around the island." *Thank goodness,* Katie thought, hoping that she didn't look too pleased.

"The Zelts are taking the booze cruise too," Mark said.

"Let's hope they don't throw their clothes overboard," Edwin said, and everyone chuckled.

Katie recalled the cruise director's outrageous tales of drunken passengers returning from island cruises. One elegant couple, full of rum, had a glorious battle on deck, ending only when they had thrown overboard every item of clothing they had brought except the clothes on their backs. Expensive evening gowns and suits had floated away in the Caribbean. Amazingly, after sobering up, they had laughed it off.

She noticed Bob watching her and glanced away. What was he thinking about last night? After seeing David and Giselle observing them from the upper deck, she had pretended not to have noticed. When she had looked again, they were gone. Terrified that she wouldn't find Giselle in the cabin, she had talked Bob into staying up for the midnight barbecue, although he hadn't required much urging. Fortunately, when she returned to the cabin, Giselle was sound asleep.

Katie smiled at Bob as the waiter brought her a breakfast menu. "Where's David?"

"Handling some tour group problems," Bob answered. "He's meeting us out on the dock. If he can't get away in time, he said that we should go on."

She fervently hoped that David would be there. She didn't want to be alone with Bob today. Her feelings about both men were growing increasingly complex.

Later, walking down the gangway into the dazzling sunshine, she was pleased to see David waving to them from the midst of the taxis assembled to transport cruise passengers on tours.

"It's a good thing that we're the only cruise ship in today," Bob said as they made their way through the traffic jam to the cab that David was holding for them. Ella and Edwin were already settled in the front seat.

"Good morning," David said, helping her into the back seat of the black cab, and smiling as if nothing of consequence had changed between them.

His eyes moved over her, approving her white slacks and deep turquoise T-shirt with its softly curved short sleeves and scallops at each side seam. She had brushed her hair back, and her only jewelry was a white bracelet and white enameled hoop earrings.

She climbed into the middle of the back seat, camera dangling around her neck again. In the front seat, Ella and Edwin chatted happily with the native driver. Bob got in on one side of Katie, David on the other, and she wondered uneasily what the day might bring.

When they were all settled, the driver turned to the back seat. "Good day," he said. "My name is Adam, and I bid you welcome to St. John's, Antigua." His clipped British accent was delightful. He turned to his driving and maneuvered through the traffic.

Katie felt David slip his arm casually over the back of the seat behind her and pretended not to notice. Did he think that he could pick up with her as if nothing had happened yesterday? Didn't he know how abandoned she had felt when he left with Giselle?

She recalled, too, that she had spent most of the evening with Bob, and others might have misinterpreted that. Perhaps David had felt betrayed when he had seen them together. Or perhaps he didn't care.

She felt curiously torn, sitting between them. Each of the men seemed to be wearing the same musky aftershave, and the fragrance sent her senses reeling. There was Bob's strong tanned arm close to hers on one side; on the other, David's arm around the back of the seat.

Darting a glance at David's angular profile as he looked out the window, she reminded herself that he had not made any promises to her. She wondered if he ever would.

Bob seemed more open, more vulnerable than David. Or was that only because of his present separation?

She tried to concentrate on what Adam was saying as they took a shortcut through St. John's, the capital and major city of the island.

"When Columbus first saw this island, he be glad he was worshiping in a church in Spain, Santa Maria of Antigua. So he calls this island Antigua."

Katie felt David's fingers drifting down the seat back to touch her shoulder. She turned to him, but he was looking out at the passing scenery, seemingly oblivious of her.

Adam continued his talk. "We are in the Leeward Islands, formerly the British West Indies, but now we got the independence. Over the years comes along Sir Francis Drake, then those pirates, then Lord Nelson . . ." Adam paused.

"You still have pirates around?" Edwin asked, smiling.

Adam laughed uproariously. "No more pirates here," he said. "Only tourists drinking up too much rum."

They all chuckled.

The suburbs of St. John's behind them, they drove through verdant countryside and small villages with names like All Saints and Liberta.

"What are those trees, Adam?" Katie asked. The dense trees with enormous tropical leaves supported round, green fruit far larger than grapefruit.

"Breadfruit," he replied. "Most every house got one of those trees. We fry breadfruit and mash 'em and eat 'em every which way."

As they drove at a leisurely speed through the countryside, the sun beamed on old sugar cane plantations and cotton fields. There was a mystical feeling in the luminous morning as natives, dressed in their bright Sunday best, walked the road to their small churches. There was a poignancy to the scene and a sense of unreality, too, as if the pages of National Geographic had sprung to life.

In the next village, the sound of fervent gospel singing filled the warm air. The small church was set back from the road among palm and breadfruit trees, its doors and windows open wide to catch the morning breezes.

"May we stop to listen?" David asked.

Adam pulled over to the side of the road and turned off the motor.

The small congregation was singing "What a Friend We Have in Jesus" with a hint of calypso in the musical accents. But there was something more. She listened intently.

"What a privilege to carry . . . everything to God in prayer . . . Oh, what peace we often forfeit . . . oh, what needless pain we bear . . ."

David opened his car door, getting out to stand in the breeze.

What is he thinking with that inscrutable look on his face? Katie wondered as she slid to the edge of the seat and swung her legs out into the sunshine.

"All because we do not carry everything to God in prayer . . . Have we trials and temptations? Is there trouble anywhere? We should never be discouraged . . . take it to the Lord in prayer."

Her eyes closed at the transcendent joy in their voices. The beauty of faith, of love rang in their voices. She recalled Gran Lucy saying that God rejoices in prayers sent on wings of love.

"Can we find a friend so faithful, who will all our sorrows share? Jesus knows our every weakness . . . take it to the Lord in prayer."

The hymn drifted through the balmy air with such overpowering love that Katie's spirit rose with it, feeling a benediction with the harmonious "Amen."

Adam started the motor. "We've got to move on."

Katie thought that if she saw or heard nothing else of interest all day, just the sound of love in those voices would have been well worth the trip. She wished that she had such faith.

David said nothing as he climbed back into the taxi, although he seemed moved.

"What beautiful voices," Ella said to the driver.

"Oh, yes," he said as they pulled away. "And they mean what they sing."

They rode in contemplative silence for a long time. They drove through several other small towns, then pulled into a long private driveway that ended in a great parking lot full of taxis and their fellow passengers from the ship.

"Clarence House," Adam announced. "Named for the Duke of Clarence who became King William IV. It be the governor's country house now. Princess Margaret spent some of her honeymoon right here."

David helped Katie out of the taxi. Her eyes quickly moved away from his, and she fixed them firmly on the one-story house. Its screened verandas and shutters made it look more like plantation houses she had seen in pictures than a residence for royalty. With Bob on the other side, they followed a native guide who led them through the house, explaining the unique features and pointing out antiques brought from England.

"Isn't it lovely?" Katie whispered.

"If you like this, you should see the country houses in Europe," David answered, making her feel hopelessly naïve, although she was certain that it wasn't his intent.

The guide told humorous anecdotes about the illustrious

people who had been guests of Clarence House as he led the group through the rooms, ending in back with the outdoor kitchen.

Outside, David and Bob seemed to be vying for the chance to seat Katie in the taxi, and she sensed a new tension between them, fearing that she was the cause. She was glad when the cab took off again, and she could lean forward to chat with Ella to avoid the silence growing between the two men.

"Next is Lord Nelson's Dockyard," Adam said. "Lots of boats still in there."

Minutes later, he parked outside the entrance to the Dockyard and explained where to meet them later.

Getting out of the cab, Katie joined Ella. Ahead, there was a long brown brick wall hung from one end to the other with a clothesline full of colorful dresses for sale. Perhaps twenty native women stood waiting for them in the shade of nearby trees.

"Hello, dearies," a buxom dress vendor flashed a toothy smile. "Buy dresses from me first. I give you good price."

"Not now, thank you," Katie said as they walked on.

The woman pressed forward. "You remember my name, Pearla."

"One size fits all," the next vendor said as she tried to force a bright blue dress with great white flowers emblazoned across it into Katie's arms. "Beautiful dress for beautiful lady!"

"It is," Katie said, trying to get away without much success.

Edwin stepped forward. "We're not letting our women do any buying," he said in such a gruff, chauvinistic voice that Katie laughed.

His ploy to avoid the overzealous dress vendors worked temporarily until they met some women selling tamarind seed and bead jewelry from tables, tree stumps, and their own brown arms, which they used as display racks.

Ella stopped to admire an elderly woman's armful of tamarind necklaces and discussed the price.

"How much for ten of these?" she asked.

"Oh, no!" Edwin moaned.

Edwin began to object, but Ella said firmly, "We don't let our men interfere with our shopping. I'll take all ten of them."

Everyone laughed so that Edwin gave in with a helpless wave of his arms. When the sale was consummated, he asked, "What on earth are you going to do with ten of those necklaces?"

Ella didn't look at all flustered as she put the jewelry into the commodious, yellow canvas handbag that matched her skirt. "I'm collecting gifts for the international table at the church bazaar."

"Well," Edwin said, "ask a silly question . . . No wonder you brought that shopping bag of a purse along!"

The vendors stood listening and laughing, spreading merriment in waves all around them.

Katie was still amused as they entered the two-hundred-year-old dockyard, then amazed to find that the harbor in the distance was full of modern yachts—everything from eighteen footers to a two-hundred-footer with a small helicopter on the forward deck.

As Katie wandered along between David and Bob on the broken sidewalk, her shoe caught on a chunk of concrete, throwing her forward.

David grabbed her.

"Thank you!" she said, regaining her balance.

"I don't intend to let you break your neck," he said, tucking her hand firmly in his arm.

She looked up and noticed the muscle tensing in his jaw,

a look of determination on his face. She thought that Bob saw it, too, before he walked away to inspect an old sundial.

Pulling out her camera, Katie took pictures of the historical buildings. Dark brick trimmed in white, they had blue shutters at the windows. Near the water, still standing, were giant stone pillars of what had once been a two-storied boathouse and sail loft. There were enormous old cauldrons for boiling pitch and old cannons sunk into the ground as bollards.

"Let's take a look in the naval museum," David suggested, and they moved ahead of the others to an ancient building. After a while he said, "I'm sorry about yesterday . . . about deserting you at St. Maarten."

When he looked at her so remorsefully, she was speechless. "You owe me no apology," she finally answered. After all, there was no reason for him to be at her side constantly. She was the one who had grown to expect it. No doubt Giselle expected his attention too.

As the doors creaked shut behind them in the musty museum, she realized that they were alone. David turned to her, his brown eyes full of warmth. "Katie . . ." His arm moved around her, and at his touch, she melted. Voices drifted in as the doors creaked open again, admitting other tourists, and David moved away, his eyes darkening with disappointment.

She moved on around the exhibits with David, berating herself for her foolishness. How could she have been so anxious for him to hold her again? He was obviously not to be trusted, and she was foolish to yield to her fickle emotions.

Nevertheless, she wandered through the museum, far more aware of David's presence than of the two-hundred-year-old muskets, pulleys, sextants, uniforms, and original drawings of the buildings. Studying a miniature model of the old shipyard from Lord Nelson's time, she thought of the English women who had been left behind to await the sailors' return from the sea.

Later, at the Admiral's Inn, an old brick restaurant with outdoor tables and chairs, Katie and David stopped for refreshments. A verdant lawn extended to the turquoise bay. There were old pillars of a bygone boathouse and, beyond the water, green hills seemed to climb to the bright blue sky.

They carried their glasses of punch outside, sitting down in the shade of a willow tree. A slight breeze stirred the willow leaves, and birds twittered overhead.

"What a beautiful place," Katie said. The grounds, studded with palm trees and the giant stone boathouse pillars, drew them back into another era. She sipped the cool fruit punch, then leaned back to enjoy the breeze.

"May we join you?" Edwin asked as he, Ella, and Bob approached the table with their glasses. Katie noticed that Bob took the seat at the end of the table farthest from her, although he didn't seem angry, only reflective.

Fifteen languorous minutes later, they climbed into Adam's taxi, settling down for the rest of the morning tour.

Katie sat uneasily between David and Bob again, although there was plenty of interesting scenery to divert her. She took pictures of native villages and tropical countryside with banana tree plantations and coconut palms. Ruins of sugar refineries from earlier times protruded like crumbling towers on overgrown hillsides. On the road, black boys rode scrawny donkeys, some carrying enormous clusters of ripe bananas on their heads.

As they returned to St. John's and pulled up by the Golden Renaissance, David made arrangements for Adam to wait while they changed into their bathing suits aboard ship. The cruise director had recommended a swim at Buccaneer Cove and the famous lobster dinners served at the beach.

At Buccaneer Cove, David, Bob, and Edwin walked on ahead as Katie and Ella scuffed along the sandy path leading through a thick grove of trees to the beach.

"What is going on with the three of you?" Ella whispered.

Katie shrugged unhappily. "I wish I knew."

"If I'd taken you for such a man-maddening character, I would never have let Edwin close to you," she said, her eyes twinkling.

"It's not funny," Katie sighed. She liked both David and Bob, although David was the one who had set her head spinning. But it was difficult to trust him—or herself when she was near him!

A native band pounded out a calypso beat, filling the soft air with its sensual rhythms as Katie stepped out to the white sandy beach. Distant peninsulas tamed the turquoise sea here, slowing the waves so that they whispered into the cove, lapping at the fine sand. Small sailboats lay at anchor to one side, near a residential area, but otherwise the meandering shortline was as pristine as it might have been in the beginning of time.

"It's glorious," Ella said. "All we need now is some of that lobster they were talking about."

"Where do you ladies want to sit?" Edwin called back to them over the calypso music.

"In the sun!" Katie said.

"Shade!" Ella countered.

They found a place to suit everyone next to a round wooden picnic table under a sprawling shade tree. It was close enough to the steel band, yet far enough removed that they wouldn't be deafened by the music.

Katie slipped out of her beach robe, and ran across the creamy sand, splashing into the turquoise water. She swam out until she felt alone in the exquisite beauty of the cove.

Treading water, she found David and Bob rapidly closing the distance between them.

"Where did you learn to swim like that?" Bob asked.

"A swim team," David guessed.

She laughed. "Right. A long time ago it seems . . . in high school."

Later, when they swam back to the beach, they were famished, and the Goodmans were already exclaiming over their giant buttery lobsters.

"I'll get ours," Bob said, taking off for the rustic beach restaurant.

Katie dried herself, then spread the oversized towel on the hot sand. Lying down sleepily, she watched David spread his towel beside hers. She closed her eyes against the blazing sun.

Katie drifted between consciousness and sleep. She heard the steel band, the voices all around her, yet Giselle's face came clearly into view. The blond beauty stood between Katie and David, scornfully flinging Katie aside.

"He loves me!" Giselle screamed at her. "David loves me!"

"No!" Katie announced. "No, it's not true!"

Jerking awake, she opened her eyes and saw David watching her.

"What on earth were you dreaming? What isn't true?" he asked.

Katie blinked, shaking her head. "Just a nightmare," she said gratefully. But it seemed so real.

Across the beach, Bob was bringing their lobster dinners. "They look fantastic!" he called out.

Katie stood up groggily and slid onto the bench by the table. "How long did I sleep?" she asked David. It seemed as if the nightmare had repeated itself hundreds of times.

"Ten or fifteen minutes," he answered.

She wondered what other monsters lurked in her head as Bob placed before her the succulent white meat, swimming in hot butter. She dug in with her fingers and feasted until the reality of the dream faded.

Ella and Edwin, satiated with the sun and full meal, leaned back to listen to the band.

When Katie finished, she sat back between David and Bob, watching the young red-shirted natives casually beating out the sensual rhythm under a canopy of bright green trees. Except for the tension that she was obviously creating between David and Bob, she wished that time could stand still.

All too soon David said, "Time for a last swim. We have to be back on the ship at three forty-five."

She walked slowly out to the water, wanting to fix this scene in her memory forever. She turned to Bob. "I can never thank you enough for bringing me on this trip."

"All part of being a tour director," Bob said and raced ahead into the water.

"Aren't you going to swim?" David called back to her.

She blinked. "Race you!" she shouted.

An hour later, they were back on the Europa Deck of the Golden Renaissance, watching the island of Antigua growing smaller. The twin spires on the cathedral in downtown St. John's reminded Katie that they had not had nearly enough time to explore the small island. "Someday I'd like to come back," she said.

"Perhaps you will. Giselle's working out Caribbean land tours for clients now," David said.

At the mention of her name, the nightmare returned, obscuring the beauty of the day and the little town fast disappearing below the horizon, until there was only a green hilly island in the distance and a sky full of great white clouds above.

Suddenly the one dark cloud overhead gave way, releasing warm drops of rain. Everyone scurried for cover until she, David, and Bob were the only passengers remaining at the railing. Sun filtered through the swirling clouds, beaming through the rain.

For a moment, Katie wondered why there was no rainbow. Then there it was—a brilliant bow of bright colors reaching from the sea up through the clouds and arching to the Caribbean again. It spanned the distant island of Antigua, a symbolic promise of the future. But what . . . and with whom? Meanwhile Katie stood, transfixed—on the deck between Bob and David.

CHAPTER 10

INSIDE THE CROWDED Riviera Deck, Katie moved along slowly in the disembarkation line toward the gangway with David, Bob, and Giselle. The other passengers, refreshed from the night's rest, were eager to explore yet another of the exotic ports—Barbados. The very name of the island conjured images of tropical enchantment. Katie was determined not to let Giselle spoil this day for her.

Scanning the brochure, she noticed again the Barbados Tourist Board's recommendation that tourists "avoid scanty attire, especially in towns and churches." She hoped her yellow eyelet sundress was appropriate. Giselle, clad in very brief black shorts and a deep V-necked T-shirt, had tossed her blond pageboy and laughed at the ruling. "Why worry about it? It's our money they're after!"

From across the crowded deck, Katie saw Walt Zelt watching them. It seemed that he was always at the edges of her life lately.

"Let's have the history, Katie," Bob said. Giselle glanced up in disgust, but David appeared interested.

Katie opened the brochure and grabbed a deep breath. "The Portuguese discovered the pear-shaped, twenty-one-mile-long island in 1536 and, before sailing on, named it Barbados after the beardlike growth on the aerial roots of the hairy fig tree."

"Now there's a fascinating fact, Giselle," Bob said with a grin.

Katie read on, ignoring Giselle's exasperation. "The island was uninhabited when the English settlers arrived in 1627, although there is evidence that Arawak Indians had lived there."

She skipped the more boring details. "Barbados remained under British rule until 1966 when it became independent . . . So it's not surprising that British influence remains strong among Bajans, most of whom are descendants of African slaves brought in to work the sugar and tobacco plantations."

"No doubt we'll be riding on the left side of the road," David said as they stepped out to the gangway. "Here we go!"

The city of Bridgetown shimmering in the morning sun revealed docks, warehouses, city buildings, and roads with snarled traffic—nothing at all like Antigua or St. Maarten. So-called civilization had obviously set in.

On the dock, Giselle hailed their tour taxi. "Let's go," she said. "Why don't you sit up front, David? You'll have more leg room. And, Katie, since you're the shortest, you can sit in the middle."

Irritated, Katie scooted into the back seat. How dare Giselle assign their places as if they were children! She wondered why David and Bob put up with it. Was Giselle's ten percent ownership of the company that important to them? Was that why David had taken off with her at St. Maarten?

In moments their taxi edged through the congestion and headed into the heavy traffic of Bridgetown—driving on the left side of the street. At first Katie braced every time they turned a corner, positive they would careen into another car.

Their native driver seemed either sullen or shy, giving occasional information in a kind of pidgin English. "Bridgetown," he said, "got our own Trafalgar Square with a statue of Lord Nelson, just like London. And we got our parliament there, and the other government buildings.

"On the corner of Bay and Chelsea there, we got the George Washington house, where he visited."

Katie craned her neck to see it. "Is that it?" she asked, noticing only a cleaning establishment.

"Yes, ma'am," the driver answered. "General Cleaners now."

Bob chuckled, and David turned to smile sympathetically at her.

"I knew that Washington slept in lots of places," she said, "but I never imagined him sleeping at a cleaners."

"Travel not only broadens," David observed, "it sometimes disillusions."

"Our David is quite the philosopher today," Giselle said with an intimate look at him.

Katie glanced out Bob's window at the shops. She was not in the mood for Giselle's seductive ploys. Bob seemed terribly quiet, yawning frequently as if he had not slept well.

Later they drove by St. Michael's Cathedral near Queen's Park. "Washington went to Anglican services here," the driver said. "And here in the park we got the giant baobab tree. Over one thousand years old."

"Now that is surprising," Giselle said. "I always think of baobabs as indigenous to Africa."

Never having even heard of the trees, which Giselle

explained were the source of cream of tartar, Katie again felt naïve and untraveled. It wasn't merely her ignorance of native trees; it was a total lack of sophistication. How could she have ever imagined that David, president of a travel company, might be seriously interested in her?

She was glad when they drove north—out of the city. A little later, when they stopped at a monument dedicated to the island's first settler, she changed her mind. There, in the **tour taxi** behind them, was Walt Zelt with his wife and other Golden Renaissance passengers.

At Fortress Hill, they turned inland to the east. Although the road was narrow, there was very little traffic, and Katie relaxed. It was quiet as everyone looked out at the hilly countryside.

After a while, the driver stopped at a turkey farm for more picture-taking.

"*Let's go on to something more interesting.* We'd rather spend our time visiting places like Villa Nova," Giselle said coldly, ignoring the hurt on their driver's face.

As they drove on, Katie noticed David's keen interest as Giselle expounded on Villa Nova, a sugar cane great house from early plantation days in the Caribbean. She had studied the area extensively in a recent university class and spouted interesting, if obscure, details.

Bob leaned back, closing his eyes.

As Katie watched Giselle and David, again engrossed in conversation, she felt invisible. Tuning out their words, she listened only to the deep rumble of David's voice, her eyes roaming to the back of his head where his dark, thick hair fell into a wave several inches above his shirt collar. Suddenly she had the urge to caress his neck. Appalled, she looked aside, wondering how she could become so captivated by a man who was obviously only interested in her when Giselle was not around. It was ludicrous!

She glanced at Bob, who drifted in and out of sleep. He had been more quiet than usual this morning, more serious. She wondered if his interest in her was only loneliness because of his separation from his wife.

She reminded herself that shipboard romances were notoriously short-lived. They did not last long once the passengers returned to the realities of life ashore, leaving only beautiful memories and, more often than not, broken hearts. She must remember to protect hers.

At the Villa Nova estate, the cab driver dropped them off by the main entrance. Flowers bloomed along walkways and great trees sprawled over bright green grounds. It was an impressive place.

Noticing the Zelts just behind them, Katie tried to concentrate on the distant stone plantation house. White-trellised verandas surrounded the first floor; on the second story, the upper white shutters swung up like canopies to block out the mid-day sun, and the lower shutters folded out neatly against the dark stone.

"Exactly as a Caribbean plantation house should look," Giselle said, taking David's arm as they walked along the path to the house.

Katie said nothing and, beside her, Bob was equally silent.

Women volunteers with clipped British accents showed them through the house, pointing out the exquisite antiques.

"Villa Nova was once the home of former English Prime Minister, Sir Anthony Eden," their guide explained.

In the garden, orchids and hundreds of other exotic flowers and shrubs bloomed in a profusion of riotous color. Under an especially lush shade tree, there was a marble bath tub in which the prime minister had taken his baths. Water lilies now floated on the water.

"Now that's the right place for a tub," Walt Zelt said

from somewhere behind them. "I wouldn't mind taking my baths in the great outdoors."

Just the thought of Walt in the tub was loathsome, Katie thought.

When they climbed back into their taxi, Giselle expounded on the beauty of the house and grounds. "Didn't you enjoy it?" she asked Katie.

"It was marvelous," she said, but there seemed to be nothing more to add to Giselle's glowing comments. Moreover, she was feeling oddly nervous with Walt Zelt in the vicinity.

Later, as they pulled into the shaded parking lot next to St. John's Anglican Church, the driver said, "Be sure to see the old cemetery in back."

The church, built of massive gray stones that had blackened over the centuries, had a broad tower rising from the middle, dwarfing the main structure. Battlements on the rooflines and thickly buttressed side walls gave the aged church a look of solidity.

"Ugly old thing, isn't it?" Giselle asked as they climbed out of the taxi.

"Well, it was built in 1650," David answered.

"I suppose the thing to do is to see it anyhow," she said.

David eyed her black shorts and revealing T-shirt. "Do you think you're suitably dressed?"

Giselle, surprised by his comment, laughed, but dropped back.

Bob, who had opened one eye to observe their stop, decided to nap in the car.

Inside, the church appeared to have been renovated. Its white walls were freshly plastered, and the stained-glass windows and lacy grillwork in front of the chancel had certainly been added more recently than 1650.

Katie sat down on a wooden pew and ran her fingers

lightly over the worn wood, wondering how many thousands had prayed here over the centuries—and for what? Had they found Gran Lucy's peace—and Ella's joy?

For a time she sat quietly, trying to shut out the boisterous tourists who viewed the church as another tourist attraction and wanted only to whisk through, snapping pictures for their scrapbooks. Bowing her head, she relaxed, allowing the hallowed atmosphere to seep into her very being, quieting her soul until every distraction disappeared. *Heavenly Father*, she prayed, *I want to be as close to You as I once was. Help me to become the person You want me to be . . . I know You want me to forgive those who have caused me pain—Stan . . . David . . . even Giselle.*

She paused. She didn't *want* to forgive Giselle. That was one woman who knew precisely what she wanted and didn't mind hurting others in the process.

Father, please help me to want to forgive . . . she amended.

As voices nearby shattered the silence, she rose sadly, knowing that she was not yet ready for her prayer to be answered.

As she edged out of the pew, she was surprised to see David sitting several pews behind her, his head bowed. She had never really considered the state of his spiritual life.

She walked slowly up the middle aisle to the lacy grillwork at the chancel, admiring the narrow stained-glass windows that ended in peaks pointing heavenward. She hadn't felt as if she were pointed in that direction lately.

Someone stepped up beside her. Turning, she saw David, his eyes glowing warmly.

"To borrow your favorite word, it's lovely," he whispered.

She smiled as they stepped outside. "Very different from

our old California missions, yet born of the same kind of faith, I think."

"Shall we take in the cemetery?" he asked.

"Why not?" she answered.

The sides of the church were even blacker with age, and greenery grew against the buttresses. In back, the cemetery was a tangle of green trees, bushes, and ferns. Moss thrived among the cracked stones on vaults, headstones, and granite crosses.

"Look at this," David said, stopping near a blackened stone vault.

Under the name, the inscription read: "A native of this island and for more than forty years a resident in the colony of British Guiana. 'I am to be gathered unto my people. Bury me with my fathers.'"

Strange, Katie thought. A man who had left his island, yet wanted to be buried with his forefathers. Surely there was an interesting story behind it.

Looking up, she found David watching her. What does he want of me? she wondered. Surely he was more interested in Giselle, who had been right about one thing—on a long-term basis, he needed someone sophisticated and well-traveled.

They peered down over the thick grove of trees marching down to the deserted beaches, and the turquoise sea beyond.

"It must be the most beautiful cemetery view on earth," he said.

She nodded and busied herself taking pictures. As she started back toward the church with David, there was Walt Zelt snapping pictures that surely included her. She felt apprehensive, somehow violated.

When they reached the parking lot, Giselle handed out small candies. "Picturesque place for shopping," she said.

"Where's Bob?" Katie asked.

"Asleep on the back seat," Giselle said.

"He hasn't been sleeping much lately," David said, then reluctantly awakened him.

"Going next to Sam Lord's Castle," their driver said as they piled in.

Driving southeast, it seemed only a short time before they arrived at the Castle, a national museum and resort.

As they started down the path, Giselle took David's arm, and Katie hung back with Bob, still groggy with sleep.

"What's wrong, Bob?" Katie asked, concerned. "Something must be troubling you."

He looked out over the formal gardens of the resort, his eyes raw with pain. "I miss Suzanne," he said. "I can't get her off my mind, no matter what I do. I keep thinking that if only I had brought her, if we had had more time together . . ."

Katie glanced away. If she suggested her first thought, she would ruin forever any chances for romance she might have with him, but it seemed more important to ease his torment if she could. "It's not too late, Bob. It's never too late." She remembered his poor opinion of himself, and added: "You're a wonderful and attractive man."

"Sure," he said skeptically.

She had an inspiration. "Why don't you send a radiogram from the ship?"

"What would I say?"

"That you love her, that you'd like to try again." Katie looked at David and Giselle, wandering through the gardens. "I wish someone loved me so much that he went mooning all over the Caribbean." She forced a smile, knowing she had put an end to any possible romance with Bob. And everything with David was apparently over too.

As they caught up with David and Giselle, she said, "Well, let's hear about Sam Lord's Castle." At least she might be able to learn something of value to her career.

Giselle seemed delighted to fill them in. "Sam Lord was a pirate of sorts," she explained. "He supposedly lured ships here to his plantation by hanging lanterns on trees and even on his goats. Ship captains, thinking they were lights in a safe harbor, would founder on his beach."

Just like some girls who lure men to destruction, Katie thought.

"And for that he was knighted?" David asked.

"It seems he was!" Giselle answered with a laugh.

Strange that the pirates of the world are so often rewarded in one way or another, Katie mused.

"The important thing here, of course, is the resort," Giselle said silkily.

The world-famous resort was composed of villas set in seventy-two acres of formal gardens, with swimming pools, tennis courts, and every possible amenity. Below on the beach, turquoise waves caressed the white sandy beach.

"It's all very nice if you want to be idle," Katie said as they paused in a garden bar for a glass of punch. "But I'm afraid I'd be bored in a few days."

Giselle's brown eyes glittered. "You probably have had very little experience as a resort guest."

Katie felt as if she were cutting her own throat. "None," she answered and sipped her fruit punch. "But I do like the castle."

Giselle shook her head, her blond pageboy drifting like gossamer over her tan shoulders. "It's so gauche, Katie."

She winced, knowing that she had left herself open for that jab. She looked across the grounds to the white, two-story mansion known as Sam Lord's Castle. The house had a certain charm and elegance despite the battlements notching the rooflines, giving it a raffish look befitting a pirate pretending to be genteel. She was certain that was how

Giselle viewed her—a pretender. Gauche. And David? It no longer mattered what he thought of her.

Inside the mansion there were valuable paintings, period furniture and other antiques, which, according to Giselle, had been seized from the shipwrecks on the beach. Giselle was extremely knowledgeable and articulate, and David seemed more and more impressed.

Climbing into the cab, Bob confided, "I'm going to do it, Katie. I'm going to send the radiogram."

After lunch in Bridgetown, he was eager to get back to the ship. Since Katie did not want to interfere with Giselle's and David's plans for the afternoon, she decided to accompany Bob.

"Are you sure?" Bob asked.

"There's shopping just outside the ship near the dock," she reminded him. Before Bob could question her further, she called to David and Giselle. "We're heading back. See you later."

She tried to decipher the expression on David's face. Surprise. Nothing else.

Early the next morning as they climbed onto a tender boat for Martinique, Katie stayed with Bob, who was in far better spirits since sending the radiogram. It was too soon to expect a response from Suzanne, though he clearly felt relieved to have made an attempt at reconciliation.

In front of them David sat with Giselle, drifting ever deeper into her sensuous web, Katie thought. She tried not to look at them. As the boat moved away from the Golden Renaissance, she decided to look forward to the day ahead. She gazed out to the island of Martinique, where a centuries-old fortress lined a cliff, then to the modern city of Fort-de-France.

On the dock, Walt Zelt pressed through the crowd to them. "How about letting me ride along with you?" he asked Giselle and David. "Sondra's sick. She's staying on the ship."

Giselle paused momentarily, then agreed. "Sure. Come on."

It wasn't surprising that Sondra was sick, Katie thought. A number of the passengers had come down with flu, including Edwin Goodman. Ella was remaining with him today.

Climbing into their taxi, Katie found she had no choice but to sit in the middle of the front seat since Giselle was already settling in the back with Bob and David. Katie smiled at the friendly native driver, trying to ignore Walt who was pressing in beside her.

"We start with our countryside," the driver said as the cab took off with a shriek of tires. "Later you have time to shop in Fort-de-France."

As they turned a corner, Katie found herself thrown against Walt, who laughingly caught her and said to the driver, "You can keep that up all day."

She jerked away, glaring at him.

They drove crazily through the city, past modern office buildings as well as bustling outdoor markets displaying a colorful array of vegetables, flowers, and fruits. Here and there on the crowded sidewalks, native women wore bright native dress. From the open windows of the taxi, they heard French and a rapid Creole patois—a blend of Spanish, English, and French. Music with a subdued African beat could be heard from car radios.

"The Carib Indians named Martinique the island of flowers," the driver said, "and to this day, the magnificent flowers are one of our main attractions."

"Not to mention the beautiful women!" Walt added.

"Oh, yes!" the driver agreed. "You do know that Josephine, the Empress of France, was born here?"

"They know how to get around men, don't they?" Walt asked.

"Oh, they surely do," the driver agreed with a savvy grin.

"She sure knew how to get around Napoleon!" Walt exclaimed, and the driver laughed uproariously.

Katie was relieved when their conversation about women ended, and she concentrated on their drive through the suburbs.

Turning inland, the driver explained, "First, we are going to St. Pierre. As you might know, that whole city was destroyed in 1902 when the volcano Mount Pelee erupted. Forty thousand people were killed in that eruption."

As they drove through the misty green countryside, Katie tried to ignore Walt, but his proximity made it difficult. If he understood her angry glances, he showed no sign of retreating. She wondered if David or Bob had noticed her plight, but they were busily discussing the Wallace-Tyler tour possibilities in Martinique with Giselle.

When they finally arrived at the town of St. Pierre, Katie gratefully slid out of the front seat and hurried to the Mount Pelee museum.

"No museums for me," Walt said. "I'll meet you back here."

Inside the museum, Giselle stepped into the restroom, and David drew Katie aside. "Is everything all right?" he asked, with a worried look.

Katie backed away. Why should he care? "Just fine," she said coolly and excused herself, heading for the sanctuary of the ladies' room.

Later, in the museum, she avoided David assiduously, turning her back on him whenever he came near. The charred artifacts of the annihilated town added to her depression. When the guided tour was over, she stepped outside. David was taking Giselle's picture as she posed seductively on the museum wall with red bougainvillaea and the turquoise Caribbean for her backdrop.

When they returned to the taxi, Walt smelled of liquor. "Oh, man, that rum," he said with a boozy grin. Even the broken veins in his bulbous nose seemed redder.

They drove on through a tropical rain forest, during which Walt dozed, bobbing ever closer to Katie so that it was all but impossible for her to enjoy the tangle of tropical greenery and misty mountains. When Walt's head was nearly resting on her shoulder, she requested a picture stop.

Getting out, she ran to the nearby stream, ostensibly for a shot of the hulking green mountain through the valley. She didn't know how much longer she could endure sitting next to Walt, but when she reached the cab, everyone else was settled in the back seat, and Walt was holding the front door open for her.

Walt was awake as they drove on through the lush countryside to Balata. By now his thigh was pressed purposefully against hers. At Balata, they stopped to visit the miniature replica of Paris's Sacre Coeur of Montmartre.

"No churches for me!" Walt said, starting down the street toward the bars.

Katie was grateful to enter the cool church building and sink down on a pew alone. *Please give me the strength to get through this day,* she prayed. She felt dazed and sat for a long time before she could enjoy the simple painting in earthy Indian tones on the white arches and dome. The momentary retreat from the humidity and Walt soon ended and it was time to return.

Walt stood waiting near the cab's front door. She had to remind herself that the tour was nearly over. As he sat down beside her, she could smell the sickening stench of rum. She fixed her gaze straight ahead, sitting as far from him as possible.

On their return to Fort-de-France, they followed the coast, passing fishing villages on the white, sandy beaches. From the corner of her eye, she saw Walt's hand slowly moving closer and closer. Suddenly he spread his hand and squeezed her thigh.

Without even thinking, she stamped on his foot hard.

He removed his hand with a quiet chuckle. "Hellion, are you? I like spirit in my women!"

She could barely refrain from slapping his grinning face. If he said one more foul thing or tried to touch her again, she would hit him with all of her might. Her fury must have been obvious because he sat stiffly beside her, looking out at the scenery the rest of the way into Fort-de-France. Perhaps he wasn't willing to take chances with David and Bob so near.

In town, they set out for lunch and shopping.

Katie drew Bob aside. "I can't stand to be near that Walt another moment," she whispered. As they looked up, Walt was watching.

"I've got some shopping to do," Walt said. "See you all later."

"What's wrong?" Bob asked.

"He's . . . disgusting."

"You should have told us," Bob said. "What did he do?"

Katie shook her head. "I just want to forget about him." She saw David looking at them. "Come on," she said, managing a smile. "Let's shop."

In the stores there was colorful native jewelry made of beads and seeds. The more elegant shops offered French crystal, clothing, jewelry, and perfumes. Giselle purchased a bright Martinique caftan and brass slave bracelets. Bob, full of hope, bought a bottle of perfume for Suzanne.

"Aren't you buying anything?" David asked Katie.

She hadn't intended to, but with sudden pique held out a brass bracelet to the sales clerk. "Yes, this." She dug in her purse for money. What a fool she was to buy the first thing at hand to avoid facing him! When it was time to leave, she was even more disgusted to discover that her bracelet was identical to Giselle's.

On the tender, Katie found a seat with Bob as far from David as possible, although he was so busy discussing something with Giselle that he didn't appear to notice.

When they boarded the ship, Bob said, "Come to the radio room with me. I need you for courage."

"Do you think there will be an answer this soon?" Katie asked, hoping to soften the blow.

Leaving David and Giselle behind, Katie could barely keep up with Bob in his rush. What if there were no answer? Yet, in the radio room, an envelope was waiting for Bob. As he tore it open, Katie closed her eyes, breathing a prayer, *Please let it be good news!*

He stared at the message and burst into a wide grin, thrusting the paper in front of her eyes.

It read: "I love you too. Yes, yes, yes, yes! Love, Suzanne."

"She used all ten words!" Katie laughed.

Bob beamed. "I hadn't noticed that."

If only things had worked out that beautifully between her and David, she thought as they hurried to the Promenade Deck for a late lunch.

Half an hour later, the ship sailed, and they bade farewell to the island of Martinique.

That night at dinner, their table seemed strangely empty with the Goodmans and Zelts missing. At the last moment,

Walt ambled in alone, taking the empty seat beside Katie and grinning companionably.

"Miss me, honey?" he asked.

She glared back. "How is *your wife* feeling?"

Walt threw back his head and laughed, the smell of liquor heavy on his breath.

She wished that Bob were on the other side of her instead of Mark, who was preoccupied as usual with his bride. Across the table, she felt David's eyes on her, but every time she looked up, he was talking to Giselle.

Hurrying through her shrimp cocktail, she listened with dismay as Walt ordered a bottle of red wine for the two of them for dinner. He had obviously been drinking all afternoon as it was and ignored her "None for me, thanks."

When the waiter arrived with the wine, Katie said, "I don't care for any, thank you," but Walt insisted that the waiter pour for her too.

"It's good," Walt said, taking a hearty gulp. "Most expensive wine on the ship."

"Don't you understand?" she asked, losing patience. "I don't want any!"

He backed away, his eyes glittering with anger.

Katie ate her steak dinner quickly, hardly tasting it as she watched Walt consume the entire bottle of wine. His words slurred more and more as the wine had its effect. He thought himself clever, a delight to all women, Katie realized, although she couldn't understand why he should have that impression.

The dinner dragged on interminably. As Katie stood to excuse herself, Walt was watching her every move.

"Going to the movie, Katie?" Bob asked from across the table.

"Not tonight," she answered, "I'm tired. Think I'll wash out some clothes and write a letter, then just go to bed."

For the first time, Katie felt apprehensive as she stepped off the elevator onto the Europa Deck. Checking about, she found the corridor deserted.

Hurrying to her cabin, she considered what she might write to her grandmother, who would be hoping for nothing less than a grand romance—the answer to her prayers for Katie.

As she turned the key in the cabin door, Walt Zelt sprang from behind, muffling her cry of surprise with his hand over her mouth and shoving her roughly into the cabin.

"David!" she screamed instinctively when her mouth was free. She fell back across the bed, while Walt lurched convulsively to shut the door behind him.

"Get out of here!" ordered David as he kicked the door open against Walt.

Walt clutched his shoulder in pain, but David grabbed him by the collar, shaking him furiously. "If you ever come near Katie again . . ." He did not finish the threat, but thrust Walt from the room and slammed the door.

Katie was shivering uncontrollably, too bewildered to speak.

"Are you all right?" David asked gently.

Without warning she burst into tears and threw herself into his arms.

"I should never have left you," he said, holding her close. "After dinner, I was almost certain that he was following you, so I . . ."

"Just don't leave me," she begged. "Don't leave me, David!" She felt safe, sheltered in his arms.

"I never *wanted* to leave you," he said softly.

She pulled away slightly, looking up at him.

"I love you, Katie," he said, his brown eyes earnest.

"But . . . But I thought you and Giselle . . ."

He shook his head. "Giselle's only an old friend."

"I thought you loved *her!*" Katie half-sobbed.

He pulled her against him again. "Never," he said. "I feel sorry for her . . . but I could never love her."

Katie blinked away the tears clinging to her lashes as she nestled close. "I've been so jealous of her!"

"I have to take some of the blame for that," he sighed, "but I didn't know what else to do. You resisted me so much at first. I knew about Stan. I know what it's like when someone you love and trust is unfaithful to you . . ."

Then the rumors about his first wife Eva and the pilot in the plane crash were probably true, Katie thought.

"I knew that you wouldn't be able to trust men for a while," he added. "I was afraid of scaring you away, like that morning on the deck."

Katie held him closer, remembering how she had almost lost him, how she had all but handed him over to Giselle.

"I decided that I'd have to wait for you to make the first move," he continued, "but when you didn't . . ."

She tried to explain. "I've been so confused, David. I swore that I wouldn't fall in love with you or any other man." She searched his eyes for understanding.

"I almost waited too long," he said. "One minute longer . . ."

"But you didn't wait too long," she protested. "Oh, David, don't you know that I love you too?"

His eyes widened with amazement, then joy, and his lips moved hungrily to hers.

CHAPTER 11

IN THE MIDDLE of the night, Katie awakened, remembering the warmth of David's arms around her, his fervent kisses. As if to retrace them, she touched her lips.

"I love you, Katie," he had whispered over and over. They would meet for breakfast again, like the first morning on the ship. This time she would not run. This time he wanted to discuss something "important" before they docked at St. Thomas.

As they had walked in the moonlight on the Promenade Deck, the calypso singer had recognized them. "If you could can that happiness on your faces and sell it, you'd be rich, my friends," he said and moved on..

Katie and David had smiled at each other, barely aware of Giselle sitting in a nearby deck chair. Katie didn't care. The glamorous Miss Vallon was no longer a threat.

It was overwhelming to think that David had loved her all of this time, that he had purposely backed away, understanding her ambivalence—wanting love, but fearing the risk. She knew in her heart that it was true. She remembered the first day of the cruise when his kiss in the moonlight had been so full of yearning, so full of love—then the next morning when she had fled in confusion.

Katie wandered in and out of sleep into the morning hours. When she finally awakened, it was six o'clock. Sitting up, she vaguely recalled Giselle coming in during the night, but now her bed was rumpled and empty. At least the bathroom was available, Katie thought, standing and stretching luxuriously.

Wanting to look her best for David, she chose her slim white linen skirt and the silky scoop-necked violet blouse with short drifting sleeves.

Pulling on her white sandals, she thought about the wonderful day together they had planned. The ship would begin disembarking passengers on St. Thomas at eight. They would take the Coral World Island tour in the morning, then shop the afternoon away.

She glanced into the mirror. Her face glowed, her eyes danced; she looked like a woman in love. Though it was too early for perfume, she daubed a drop of Joy behind each ear and was encircled once more by the fragrance of flowers.

She looked at her watch. Only six-thirty. She smiled. How anxious she was to see him again. Picking up her white canvas handbag, she decided to go to the Promenade Deck.

As she stepped into the elevator, she was surprised to see Bob.

"You're up early," she said. "Expecting another radiogram?"

He smiled sleepily. "No, I'm expecting Suzanne."

"You're joking!" Katie said.

"I called her last night, and she's going to meet me in Martinique. I'm flying back there this afternoon."

The elevator doors opened for Katie's floor. "Bob! I'm so happy for you!" She left him, beaming as widely as he.

She felt incredibly happy. Not only had things worked out beautifully for her and David, but also for Bob and Suzanne.

Starting down the corridor, she suddenly recalled that she had forgotten her St. Thomas shopping guide. She would need it for the shopping expedition. Returning to the Europa Deck, she hurried down the corridor and, opening her door, noticed that Giselle wasn't back yet. Grabbing her guidebook, she hurried out again.

As she passed David's cabin, the door opened. At first she refused to believe her eyes, but there was no mistaking it. Giselle! Giselle, wearing her short beige nightie and filmy robe, was just leaving. And David was right behind her in blue pajamas, his brown eyes sleepy, his hair tousled. When he saw Katie, he looked aghast.

She stood rooted before them for a moment, Giselle's eyes meeting Katie's with defiance. Then Katie fled in panic.

"Katie!" David called after her.

She didn't stop, hardly knowing where she was going. She rushed outside and climbed to the next deck, then to the Sun Deck. It was vacant. She hurried to the shadow of the smokestack.

How could she have trusted him? And after all of his fine explanations last night! He had said he loved her. If this was how he showed his love, she wanted no more of it!

The stack roared dully beside her as smoke billowed into the blue sky. Her white linen skirt would be covered with droplets of oil if the wind swung the smoke over the deck, but she didn't care. She thought about the couple who had thrown each other's clothes overboard as they argued, and she knew just how they felt. At this moment she would gladly throw herself overboard.

Oh, didn't David think he was wonderfully heroic to save her from Walt Zelt! But he was infinitely worse. At least

155

Walt had not pretended he loved her. Nor was it surprising that Giselle had warned her about David's preference for sophisticated women. Obviously she had misjudged Giselle.

Dispirited, she watched the green island of St. Thomas in the distance and pulled the guidebook from her handbag. She would wait until everyone had disembarked, then she'd dash into town for a short while. She glanced dully at the book which touted St. Thomas as a shoppers' paradise. "Even if you spend the whole day shopping in the town of Charlotte Amalie," it read, "you would not be able to cover all of the shops and see what is certainly the most complete range of merchandise displayed in one small town in the whole world."

Well, she was going to see it, if only to buy a little gift for Mrs. Sanders for taking care of her plants.

As the ship neared St. Thomas, she wished that she could cry, but her heart felt cold and hard. The island was fantastically beautiful, she thought dispassionately. She stared at its green hills, the harbor full of yachts and great white cruise ships. It was a magnificent sight. But she felt nothing. Only a vast emptiness.

Remaining in the shadow of the stack until everyone was ashore, she decided that it would be safe to leave. David, Giselle, and Bob would have left for the morning tour of Coral World Island by now.

She made her way through the strangely silent ship to the gangway door. The crew stared at her curiously, but she ignored them. Swallowing hard, she walked down the gangway alone and flagged a taxi, her guidebook in hand.

Once in the waterfront town of Charlotte Amalie, she was glad that the shops were jammed with tourists; everyone was so crazed with bargain-hunting and sampling every perfume on the store counters, that she might have been invisible, floating among the shoppers like the wafting fragrances.

In a shop that carried everything from diamonds to rum, she found a tiny English china vase for Mrs. Sanders. There were so many other things to shop for—endless selections of watches, scarves, china, T-shirts, woolens, linens, jewelry, cameras, leather goods. . . . But she had spent most of her remaining money yesterday when she had insisted on repaying Bob for Gran Lucy's tablecloth. It had been far more expensive than she had dreamed.

As she paid for her purchase, she spotted David, Giselle, and Bob through the shop windows. They hadn't gone on the Coral World tour after all! She turned away quickly, unsure whether David had seen her, and rushed for the door that opened onto the next street.

Hurrying out into the narrow street, she pressed through the crowd of shoppers and looked frantically for a taxi.

"Katie!" David yelled from behind her in the street.

She ran blindly through amazed tourists whose arms cradled parcels and whose hands gripped colorful shopping bags. Finally she saw a cab and flagged it. Hopping in, she slammed the door behind her. "Golden Renaissance! Hurry!"

The driver looked at her strangely. "Yes, ma'am," he said, "although I do believe she won't be leaving until around eight o'clock tonight."

"Hurry!" she said again, glancing back.

David was nearly to her door, shouting as he ran.

She turned away and the cab moved into the heavy traffic.

"Sure does look like that man's trying to catch you," the cabbie said, glancing at her in the rearview mirror.

"Never mind!" she snapped. She was not going to listen to another thing David Wallace had to say.

"He was a nice-looking fellow," the cabbie commented.

"Oh, be quiet!" she cried, then was ashamed of herself. They rode in silence the rest of the way to the dock.

When she paid the cab driver, he shook his head. "I think you missed it with that fellow."

She whirled away, sorry that she had tipped him.

"*Bon voyage!*" he called out behind her.

Men! Katie thought. She would like to throttle all of them.

She walked angrily up the gangway, threading her way through the quiet corridors to her cabin. By the time she arrived, she was still livid with rage and disappointment.

In the cabin, she stuffed the package into her closet. If she was going to be stuck here all day, she might as well lie out in the sun, she decided, and put on her blue bathing suit and beach cover-up.

What would Gran Lucy have to say about all of this?

Katie knew the answer. Gran Lucy would pray. But she *had* prayed and everything had gone wrong again!

Full of bitterness, Katie slumped down at the dressing table and looked into the mirror, remembering the joyous face that had greeted her this morning. It had been a face glowing with love. The one peering back at her was grim with hatred.

Her heart twisted with pain. A sob escaped, then another and another. She buried her head on her arms at the dressing table, weeping uncontrollably. If God loved her the way Gran Lucy said, then how could she have been so hurt *twice?*

It was a long time before she sat up and wiped her eyes, still trembling. She knew Gran Lucy's response: "Have you surrendered everything to God, or are you still trying to run your own life?"

Tearfully she thought it over. The answer was obvious.

"You have to surrender *everything* to God—that means

your past, your present, *and* your future!" Gran Lucy would have said firmly.

"Then I surrender!" Katie wailed. "I give it all to you, God! I give up my resentment toward Giselle and my anger at Walt Zelt!"

"And David?" Gran Lucy seemed to ask.

It broke her heart, but she answered firmly, "David . . . I give up David!"

"But do you *forgive* them?"

Katie knew that she must deal with forgiveness, that it was the key to the elusive peace and joy she had sought. "Yes," she whispered. "I do forgive them."

Gran Lucy wouldn't let up. "But you must forgive Stan, too, you know."

Katie sat straighter, incredulous. "How do you know whether I forgave Stan or not?" she asked aloud as if her grandmother were in the very room.

"Because you haven't trusted men ever since," Gran Lucy seemed to be saying. "You haven't even trusted Jesus."

Katie blew her nose. "Very well then," she said, mustering all the conviction she could, "I do forgive Stan too."

"And now what?" Gran Lucy continued as if Katie were still a little girl in her arms.

"Now I can pray."

Gran Lucy persevered. "*How* should you pray?"

"Joyously," Katie said, "praising Him."

Gran Lucy's voice seemed to soften with love. "And how will God answer you?"

Katie smiled as she remembered the answer her grandmother had given her so long ago. "God answers the prayers of His children on wings of love. Even in the most bitter of circumstances, if you're right with Him and ask for help, He'll give you the peace to live with a situation or

He'll deliver you from it entirely. Or sometimes He says, *Not now; someday you'll see it all come to good.*"

Katie stood up. Her reflection filled the dressing table mirror. How enraptured she had become with herself lately instead of with God! She wished that she were outside in the sunshine and fresh air where she had so often felt His presence, but she reminded herself that He was everywhere, especially in the praise of His people.

Dropping to her knees, she closed her eyes. It came to her that the perfect prayer had already been given. She took a deep breath.

Our Father, who art in Heaven, she began, feeling a small spark of warmth opening her heart to Him again.

Hallowed be Thy Name, she whispered, the warmth in her beginning to flicker and spread.

Thy kingdom come . . . Thy will be done . . . It doesn't matter about my will, Father, she thought, aglow with love.

When she finished, she knew that she had never really meant those words before. Now she truly wanted only His will. It didn't matter about Stan; it didn't matter about David. If it was God's will that she should never marry, she was willing to accept it.

She washed the tears from her face, and her heart grew more and more peaceful. It occurred to her that she had loved Stan more than God. She had made an idol of him, expecting far more of him than any man could give. That was one mistake she did not intend to make again.

As she let herself out of the cabin, she decided that it was a good time to count her blessings. For one, this cruise . . .

"Katie!"

She glanced down the corridor. It was David!

He and Giselle walked toward her, laden with packages. David looked grim; Giselle, uncertain.

"I'd like to talk with you," he began.

"Fine," she answered with such serenity that it surprised her.

Giselle raised an elegant eyebrow. "Didn't I warn you?" she asked.

"Yes," Katie said quietly. "You did. You implied that I was an innocent, and that you and Eva were more David's type—on a long-term basis." Once the words were out of her mouth, she realized that she had answered a question that Giselle had put to David.

He looked at Giselle. "And you warned me that all Katie cared about was my money." He glanced at Katie.

She gasped. "If anything, David, I considered your money an obstacle between us. You're so knowledgeable . . . you've seen so much of the world . . . I couldn't imagine your really being interested in anyone so . . . so inexperienced."

Giselle quickly unlocked the cabin door. "Excuse me, I have to pack," she said, but her departure went unnoticed.

"You might have trusted me a little more," he said quietly. "Edwin Goodman became much worse during the night, and we had to help Ella make arrangements to get him to the hospital in St. Thomas this morning."

"Oh, no!" Katie cried.

"It's not as bad as the ship's doctor suspected at first, but Edwin's going to have tests for a few days. Giselle will stay here with Ella until he is well enough to fly home."

"If only you had told me," she said. "You must have known how it looked to me with Giselle coming out of your cabin in her nightie and you . . ."

"You took off running too fast," David protested. "I tried to find you. I searched the whole ship."

How stupid she had been. "I'm sorry, David. I just went crazy when I saw the two of you like that."

"I guess I should be flattered," he said.

"But why didn't you tell me about Edwin?"

"Bob and I thought you'd had a bad enough time last night with Walt Zelt. And when Bob knocked on your door this morning, Giselle answered."

"I guess I didn't hear it," Katie sighed.

He caught a deep breath. "The truth of the matter is that selfishly I didn't want anything or anyone to interrupt our happiness."

Katie reached for his hands, and they stood silently for a moment in the hallway.

"We had a lot to work out with Giselle too," he added. "She's going to set up a Caribbean affiliate travel agency here."

"That's what she wants?" Katie asked, amazed.

"That's what she wants."

"Since she can't have you?"

The color in his face deepened. "She didn't put it that way. But I suspect that she has contributed heavily to the complications between us. Seems I'm too trustful of women again, and you're too distrustful of men."

"I'm sorry," Katie said. "Giselle told me you needed someone like her, so when I saw the two of you together, I assumed the worst."

"Would I have arranged to bring you on this tour if that's what . . ." He stopped, appalled at his transparency.

"*You* arranged the cruise for me, David?"

He looked down sheepishly. "I've admired you for a long time, Katie," he said. "Mrs. Sanders at your apartment building knew. I drive her home from church on Sundays . . ."

So that's where she had seen his yellow Porsche before! "But how did you know I lived there?"

"I saw you one Sunday morning and asked Mrs. Sanders about you. She told me when you broke up with Stan."

David colored again. "I'm afraid that I talked her into letting me know when you returned from your grandmother's. Then I had Bob call to offer you the job."

"Oh, David," she whispered, and he caught her against him.

"I love you, Katie," he said. "I've loved you for a long time, I think since the first time I saw you years ago."

Looking up at him, she saw the same glow in his eyes that she had noticed after he'd prayed in the church in Barbados. She suddenly knew in her heart that he had been praying about her there, that he would never knowingly hurt her, that she had only to reach out . . .

"Oh, David," she whispered, "I love you too."

"I didn't think there was anyone like you left in the world," he murmured huskily. "When I was healed from that accident, I never thought I'd pray so fervently for anything again as I've prayed for you."

He is a Christian! Katie exulted. *And not just a Sunday Christian. He believes in prayer.* He had prayed for her! He had waited patiently for her!

"It's the prince and the princess," piped a little voice in the corridor. "They're hugging!"

David tousled the boy's hair as the children passed by. "I can see our children already. . . . A little girl like you . . ."

"Our children?" Katie asked.

"I've always wanted children. Don't you?"

"Oh, yes, David!"

He kissed the top of her head. "God willing, we'll have them. There's time . . ." Suddenly changing his tone, he said happily, "There's even time for a shopping expedition!"

She waited for him to explain, but he only stood there smiling down at her. "Anything special in mind?" she teased.

"An engagement ring?" he replied hopefully. "I can't bear to have you run away again. And St. Thomas is said to have some of the most beautiful gems in the world."

She hugged him. "And would we have time to see Edwin and Ella at the hospital?"

"If you can change in a hurry."

"Five minutes?" she asked before truly realizing that he had proposed.

Instead of responding, he lifted her and whirled her around in the corridor.

"Do you know that you've just agreed to marry me?"

"I didn't think that you'd even need an answer," she replied joyously, "but, yes, David . . . oh, yes!"

When his lips met hers, the wondrous prayer of thanksgiving filling her heart seemed to soar higher and higher. Like her joy, it ascended on wings of love.

MEET THE AUTHOR

ELAINE S. SCHULTE was born and raised in Crown Point, Indiana, and graduated from Purdue Iniversity. She has written hundreds of short stories and articles that have appeared in magazines and newspapers around the world. Her first novel, *Zack and the Magic Factory,* appeared on television. Her most recent novel, *Whither the Wind Bloweth,* is for young adults. She lived in Belgium for several years and has traveled extensively in Europe, the Middle East, Africa, and North America. She resides with her husband in Rancho Santa Fe, California. They have two sons in college.

About *On Wings of Love,* Mrs. Schulte says, "Several years ago I left for a Caribbean cruise with no thought of using the background for a novel. I'd just sent off galleys for another book and needed a rest. Yet after several days at sea, the characters of Katie and David came to me walking the decks, holding hands in the sunshine, embracing in the moonlight. Then came Gran Lucy, Bob Giselle, the Goodmans, and the Zelts. After the cruise their story unreeled so persistently that I had to put aside my novel in progress. The story of Katie and David quite literally came to me on wings of love."

Serenade Books are inspirational romances in contemporary settings, designed to bring you a joyful, heart-lifting reading experience.

Other Serenade books available in your local bookstore:

#1 ON WINGS OF LOVE, Elaine L. Schulte
#2 LOVE'S SWEET PROMISE, Susan C. Feldhake
#3 FOR LOVE ALONE, Susan C. Feldhake
#4 LOVE'S LATE SPRING, Lydia Heermann
#5 IN COMES LOVE, Mab Graff Hoover
#6 FOUNTAIN OF LOVE, Velma S. Daniels and Peggy E. King.

Watch for the Serenade/Saga Series,
historical inspirational romances,
to be released in January, 1984.